LAYER

ANALYSIS

LAYER ANALYSIS

A PRIMER OF ELEMENTARY
TONAL STRUCTURES

GERALD WARFIELD

DAVID McKAY COMPANY, INC.
NEW YORK

Layer Analysis: A Primer of Elementary Tonal Structures

Copyright © 1976 by David McKay Company, Inc.

Book production by Music-Book Associates
Manufactured in the United States of America

LIBRARY OF CONGRESS CATALOGING IN PUBLICATION DATA

Warfield, Gerald.
    Layer analysis.

    1. Music—Analysis, appreciation.   I. Title.
MT6.W188L4   780'.15   75-27070
ISBN 0-679-30297-2

ACKNOWLEDGMENTS

Gratitude is due the readers who have assisted me with this book in its several drafts. In particular I would like to thank Fred Nicholson, whose thoughtful and penetrating comments have been invaluable. I am also indebted to Arthur Komar and to one of my most valuable teachers at Princeton: Godfrey Winham. For their helpful review of the final manuscript I would like to mention Peter Westergaard and Richmond Browne. For the final preparation of the manuscript and further perceptive suggestions I wish to thank John Selleck.

TO THE MEMORY OF MY FATHER,
GEORGE ALEXANDER WARFIELD

HOW TO USE THIS BOOK

This book is designed to be used in two different ways:

I. AS A TEXT

It is geared for undergraduates, preferably after they have had at least some exposure to basic harmony or counterpoint. It is brief enough to use as an adjunct text in sophomore harmony classes and yet detailed enough (if augmented by the extra readings suggested in Appendix C) to serve as the sole text for an analysis course. The material is presented so that it may either precede or follow a study of musical form.

> All the exercises are printed twice. The student is encouraged to "work out" the exercises on the first set of answer sheets and then recopy them onto the second set located in the back of the book. This set can be torn from the book and turned in to the instructor.

II. AS A BRIEF EXPLANATION OF SOME OF THE BASIC IDEAS OF SCHENKER ANALYSIS

If one simply wants an introduction to Schenker-type analysis, read the Introduction, Chapters 1, 3, 6, 12, Appendix A, and Appendix B. The other chapters can be skipped or skimmed as needed.

Although this is not a literal presentation of Schenker's analytical techniques, I feel that the most important features of his approach to analysis have been preserved (i.e., prolongation technique, discrete background lines, and, of course, layers). Schenker's concept of the *Ursatz,* which I regard as a less important aspect of his work, is dealt with in the last chapter. Many of the comparatively recent revisions of "Schenker technique" have been freely incorporated into this text. The only original contribution of the present text is the layer notation, a more concise notation having been found to be an indispensable aid in teaching elementary analytical techniques of this type.

Most of the examples are from the keyboard literature or from the accompaniments of songs. This is to enable the reader to play them (most are easy) in their *original* form. It is, in fact, very important to play all the examples. Analysis is not merely a manipulation of notation. It is a representation of how we hear (i.e., understand) music; and it is vital that the reader establish maximum relationship between the sounds and the analyses.

INTRODUCTION

Layer analysis is a method whereby the underlying contrapuntal fabric of a piece of music is displayed. The origins of this method lie in the theoretical works of Heinrich Schenker, an Austrian music theorist who lived from 1868 to 1935. The principles of layer analysis are applicable to all tonal music regardless of style—folk and popular music are often easier to analyze in this manner than classical or concert music—and extensions of this method are applicable to many types of non-tonal music, both Western and non-Western.

One expects an adequate analysis to reveal significant structural aspects of a piece of music. It is not often realized, however, that much of what is discovered through such an analysis serves merely as added explanation or confirmation of one's intuitive understanding of a composition or of music in general. Even people who claim to know nothing about music can remember melodies and distinguish wrong notes in subsequent performances. In a perceptual psychological sense this is a highly complex phenomenon. Thus even if one's only exposure to music has been as a listener, it is likely that one's understanding of music (in this respect) is nevertheless at a relatively advanced level.

The fact that music can be (and *is*, most of the time) understood intuitively is evidence that principles underlie it that make it particularly susceptible to human perception. People learn through patterns, relationships, and groupings. As an example, try memorizing a random, meaningless string of words; how much easier it is to remember sentences. The notes of a tonal composition as they go by are not a random series of sounds. They are highly organized, and any listener accustomed to tonal music interprets them in these terms whether he is conscious of it or not. Analysis will help one to understand the underlying structures of music, i.e., the relationships between the notes that cause musical compositions to "make sense."

Most students of tonal analysis have reading ability and performing experience as well. For them, analysis or theory is analogous to studying the grammar of a language that they already comprehend. Such study provides deeper understanding of what they already know and, at the same time, provides a systematic method for assimilating further information.

Counterpoint, as has often been maintained, is the basis of all tonal music. However, in order to make this clear, the principles of counterpoint must be sufficiently generalized. Traditionally, counterpoint is thought of in conjunction with style, so that, for example, in a counterpoint class one might study methods for the composition of an 18th-century fugue. Layer analysis reveals a type of counterpoint stripped of major stylistic characteristics: a counterpoint general enough to form the basis of a Chopin mazurka, a Joplin rag, a Beethoven symphony, or a song by Paul Simon.

Of course, each type of music analysis attempts to display what it defines as the most meaningful or significant relationships within a piece of music (and no one type has all the answers). The approach of layer analysis is to expose the contrapuntal skeleton of a piece of music. The results should be a clear demonstration of how all the notes of a tonal composition are related to one another, how *every* pitch forms a part of the complete contrapuntal whole.

CONTENTS

LAYER ANALYSIS

CHAPTER 1

SOME PRELIMINARY OBSERVATIONS

A. REPEATED NOTES

An analysis is a way of making something simpler, that is, simplifying something so that certain relationships are easier to see. *Arriving* at a suitable analysis may be difficult, but the results should always be simpler than the phenomenon itself.

As a first step toward the simplification of passages we wish to analyze, we shall begin with the removal of repeated notes. This is a basic operation and will eventually be taken for granted in most of the analyses we do.

There is evidence in many compositions that composers have been aware of the close relationship between passages containing repeated notes and those same passages *without* the repeated notes. In the last movement of Beethoven's Symphony No. 7 the following melody appears:

mm. 26-30

EXAMPLE 1

which is soon reiterated in the following way:

mm. 34-38

EXAMPLE 2

The latter is obviously a slightly more complex version of the former.

Songs are often written with alternative repeated notes to accommodate the extra syllables of subsequent verses, and this is not thought to substantially change the melody. In the following example by Paul Simon these extra repeated notes are shown by the smaller note size:

1

PAUL SIMON: "Scarborough Fair/Canticle," mm. 33-36

"Scarborough": © 1966 Paul Simon. Used with the permission of the publisher.

EXAMPLE 3

Haydn, in the first variation of the second movement of his *Surprise Symphony* (Symphony No. 94), wrote the sixteenth-note variation melody shown in Example 4A below. The theme from which this variation was derived is shown in 4B. Notice the relationship between B and A; B is simpler because there are fewer repeated notes. One can create an even simpler passage by reducing out *all* adjacent repeated notes. This yields the "analytical layer" shown in 4C.

EXAMPLE 4

Compare the figure in 4C to the figures in 4A and 4B. 4C has no tangible existence in the composition itself, yet it is a skeletal outline that underlies both the theme (B) and the variation (A). (Although we can consider C to be an analytical layer in its own right, the layers we will be constructing will usually show more than just the deletion of repeated notes.)

B. "BACKGROUND" COUNTERPOINT

As was stated in the Introduction, tonal music is based on counterpoint, and layer analysis is a method for displaying this counterpoint. However, the kind of counterpoint we are referring to is not the kind that has to do with the relationships between two or more separate melodic lines, such as the relationships between the bass part and the soprano part of an 18th-century fugue. It is not necessarily relationships between voices, but relationships within voices, even single voices. We shall refer to this kind of counterpoint as "background" counterpoint.

One of the most important aspects of background counterpoint is that more than one line of it is usually present *simultaneously* within single melodies. Consider the following:

EXAMPLE 5

If we wished to focus on each note in succession we could think of the passage as made up of notes that follow one another in this pattern:

EXAMPLE 6

While the above relationships *do* exist (after all, the notes follow one another in that order) there is a sense in which the passage contains two simultaneous lines:

EXAMPLE 7

Both views represent ways in which we understand the passage, but the first view (Example 6) accounts only for relationships between adjacencies:

EXAMPLE 8

while the second view (Example 7) accounts for longer-range relationships between non-adjacent notes.

EXAMPLE 9

It is the representation of relationships between non-adjacent notes that begins to tell us more about the way we understand an *entire* passage, and it is precisely these longer-range relationships that layers reveal. Let us take another example:

BACH: Cantata No. 51

(Trumpet)

EXAMPLE 10

If we remove the repeated notes, as was suggested in the earlier part of this chapter, we would get the following:

EXAMPLE 11

In the second measure note the reiteration of the G's and the pattern formed by the other notes. Clearly there are two lines present: one that remains stationary on G and another that ascends by step from C up to G.

EXAMPLE 12

This means that there is a sense in which the first C in the second measure does not really "go" to the next note to which it is *adjacent,* a G, but to a note to which it is not literally (or temporally) adjacent: the D. The same is then true for the D, which goes to E, and for the E, which goes to F, etc.

This example is exceptionally clear since the notes of the moving line are emphasized by the contour of the melody and by the fact that they appear at the beginning of each beat. Linear relationships of this sort which transcend literal adjacencies are an extremely important aspect of layer analysis. What we have done is to create a simpler version (layer) of the melody in order to display these lines.

Even in such a simple analysis there are clear implications for performance. Obviously, the trumpet player must play the passage in such a way that the C *does* proceed to the D, and the D proceeds to the E, etc., through a slight crescendo or some other special treatment of these notes. Any performance which did not do this would seem mechanical and unmusical.

A layer may contain many background contrapuntal lines. The following is another Bach example which clearly displays two such lines even though only a single instrument is playing. Unlike the earlier example *both* these background lines are moving.

BACH: Suite No. 3 for Cello (Gigue), mm. 88-91

EXAMPLE 13

Background contrapuntal lines embody the primary relationships through which we understand a tonal composition. We must be careful to keep in mind, however, that the *layers* on which these lines are represented do not have a tangible existence of their own within the piece of music being examined; they are only a device for the efficient display of relationships between non-adjacent notes.

SUMMARY

A single melody will contain within it two or more background contrapuntal lines. These lines are clearly displayed in the "layers" of a layer analysis. In the notation of these lines (on the layers) repeated notes are usually deleted.

EXERCISES FOR CHAPTER 1

1. After the deletion of repeated notes the bottom background line of this passage can be represented as a sustained G, as shown in the layer below. Using eighth notes, add the top background line above the sustained G. The first two notes are already given.

BACH: Suite No. 3 for Cello (Gigue), mm. 25-31

2. There are two background lines present in the following example: one stationary and one moving. Write both on the layer below. You will have to use tied whole notes and quarter notes. The first note in each line is given.

MOZART: Sonata in E minor for Violin and Piano (K. 304)
(1st movement), mm. 104-107

3. In this example both background lines are moving. Write each on the layer below. The first two notes in each line are given.

DOMENICO SCARLATTI: Sonata No. 9, mm. 27-28

4. In the next example there are three background lines. A separate staff is provided for the notation of each (although all three combine to form the layer). The first note of each line is already given; fill in the remaining notes using only dotted quarters. Tie notes where necessary.

MOZART: Sonata in G for Violin and Piano (K. 301)
        (2nd movement), mm. 37-40

5. In this example there are four lines present (counting the bass line). In the layer below write the upper three lines (where indicated) using dotted half notes. The bass line is already given as well as the first note of each of the other lines. Tie notes where necessary.

ARTHUR FOOTE: Twenty Preludes, No. 3, mm. 3-5

6. In this measure the treble-clef part contains two lines: a line beginning on the D above middle C, and a stationary D on the octave above. On the layer fill in the moving line (marked with an arrow). You will need to use quarter notes and eighth notes. The first note is given.

BACH: Pastorale in F major, m. 33

In the above exercise, what is the relationship between the pitches of the line you filled in and the pitches of the line just below it?_____

_____

CHAPTER 2

EXERCISES IN CHORD AND INTERVAL RECOGNITION

This chapter consists entirely of exercises which review chord and interval recognition.

A. CHORD IDENTIFICATION AND INTERVALLIC STRUCTURE

1. Label each chord with Roman numerals (indicating the chord within the key) and Arabic numeral subscripts to indicate inversion (e.g., I, I_6, I_4^6, etc.). Label the chords in the first line as if they were in D major and those in the second line as if they were in A minor.

In D major:___ __ __ __ __ __ __ __ __

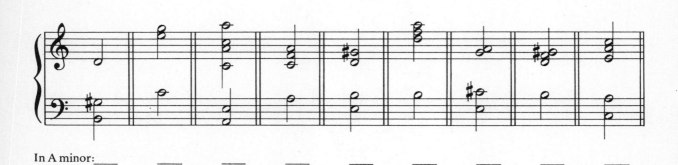

In A minor:___ __ __ __ __ __ __ __ __

2. Label the intervals marked within the following chords. Reduce each interval name to within an octave (e.g., major 10th = major 3rd). Use the abbreviations "maj." and "min."

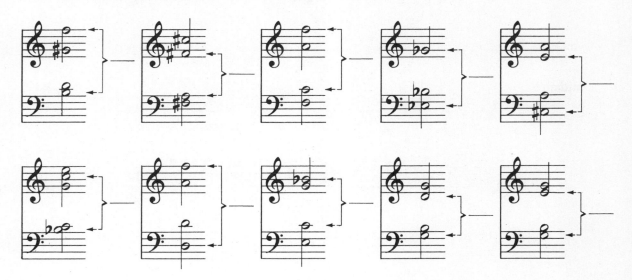

3. The initial measures of many melodies are often made up of notes from a single chord. In the space provided write the name of the chord to which the bracketed notes belong.

(a) MOZART: *The Magic Flute* (beginning)

chord:____

(b) SCHUBERT: *The Post* (beginning)

chord:____

(c) MOZART: *Bastien and Bastienne* (beginning)

chord:____

B. RECOGNITION OF CHORDS IN CONTEXT

1. Chords are easiest to identify when they appear in "block" form, as in the following example. Write the chord names (using Roman numerals) in the blanks below the staves.

BEETHOVEN: Sonata, Op. 14, No. 2 (2nd movement)

2. In the following example the bass note appears on the beat and the rest of the chord one-half beat later. Write the chord names, as before, in the blanks provided.

SCHUBERT: "By the River" ("Auf dem Flusse")

3. Sometimes chords appear in arpeggiated form (i.e., the notes of the chord are presented one at a time, not in block form nor "rolled"). In the following example a bracket is used to mark off the area, or "domain," of each chord. In the blank staves below write the chords (one for each bracket) with half notes in block form. Two are already given. Then write the names of the chords (using Roman numerals) in the blanks provided.

BEETHOVEN: Sonata, Op. 13 (3rd movement), mm. 109-112

4. Analyze the following example as directed.

 (a) Indicate the domain of each chord with brackets under the bass clef (as was done for you in the previous example). The first bracket is given.

 (b) On the staff below write out the chords for the left-hand part (the bass-clef part) in block form. Use whole notes. The first chord is given.

 (c) Write the chord names (using Roman numerals) in the blanks provided.

MOZART: Fantasia in C minor (K. 475), mm. 62-70

5. In this example only write the chord names with letters of the alphabet (A maj., E♭ min., etc.) rather than Roman numerals. Use the blanks provided. Do not show inversion.

PAUL SIMON: "A Poem on the Underground Wall," mm. 45-48

6. By writing the arpeggiations in block chords and deleting repeated notes you should be able to reduce the following entire passage to only two chords.

(a) Mark a bracket under the domain of each chord.

(b) Write the chords on the blank staves below.

BACH: *Twelve Little Preludes,* No. 3

CHAPTER 3

BACKGROUND LINES

When one speaks of "arpeggiation" the term is usually used to indicate a chord that is broken or rolled; however, in layer analysis arpeggiation refers to *any* presentation of the notes of a configuration (such as, but not necessarily, a chord) one at a time. These notes may be of any durational value, repeated, and in any order. Every example in this chapter contains arpeggiations except Example 5, where the chords are in block form. Example 1 below is entirely made up of a single configuration, which is arpeggiated.

A. BACKGROUND LINES IN GENERAL

In Chapter 1 we simplified musical passages by deleting repeated notes, thus representing all adjacent repeated notes with *single* notes. In Chapter 2 we represented all the notes of arpeggiated chords with *single* simultaneous chords. We shall combine these two methods of reduction so that *all* notes within the same arpeggiated chord (whether they are adjacent or not, or whether they are repeated or not) can be reduced to a single vertical chord. For example:

KUHLAU: Sonatina, Op. 20, No. 2

EXAMPLE 1

In the details of a musical passage it sometimes happens that arpeggiations are made up solely of chord tones. However, the notes of an arpeggiation, whether they are chord members or not, are also (although sometimes not obviously) members of contrapuntal lines. These lines, which we call background lines, extend for far longer stretches of time than single chords, and it is these lines which are being arpeggiated.

We have already seen such lines in the examples given thus far. Take, for instance, the left-hand part in the Mozart Fantasia quoted in Chapter 2. Example 2 shows the background lines marked (in the layer) with arrows and ties.

Background
lines:

Layer:

EXAMPLE 2

In a way, arpeggiation can be thought of as the articulation of the background lines one at a time, as is shown in the following diagram:[1]

Top background line

Middle background line

Bottom background line

EXAMPLE 3

Since arpeggiation articulates background lines (not just chords), dissonances which may appear in these lines can be arpeggiated too. The following example shows a typical arpeggiated figure which articulates a suspension:

1. Of course, the listener who hears such a passage for the first time will not know that two of the background lines in the second measure have moved until notes in those lines are sounded. This doesn't happen until the second and third eighth notes of that measure. The listener will then (in retrospect, and since there is no evidence to the contrary) assume the shift to have occurred on the previous downbeat. The purpose of the example, however, is only to demonstrate the lattice-type pattern of arpeggiation on the background lines.

BACH: *Twelve Little Preludes*, No. 8, m. 5

EXAMPLE 4

B. TWO CHARACTERISTICS OF BACKGROUND LINES

One primary characteristic of background lines, other than the bass line,[2] is that they *always move by step.* Thus adjacent notes in background lines will almost always be a whole step or half step apart. (This means that arpeggiation *always* indicates the presence of at least two background lines.) All background lines shown in layers prior to this point in the text have, of course, displayed this characteristic.

Another important characteristic is that background lines merge and divide freely. This means that the *number* of lines may continually vary throughout the composition. Examine, for example, the following passage. The background counterpoint is shown below on two staves. In the first measure arrows show the C and E♭ merging into the D♭ and then separating again. In the second measure E♭ and C merge again to a D♭ (in the third measure) while the low G♭ splits to form two lines.

SCHUBERT: "Hunter's Evening Song" ("Jägers Abendlied"), Op. 3, No. 4, mm. 11-13

EXAMPLE 5

SUMMARY

Background lines always move by step. Two background lines may merge or a single line may split (so long as only step motion is used). Dissonances which exist between these members of different lines may also occur as part of an arpeggiation.

2. Bass lines may move by skip, as will be explained in Chapter 7.

EXERCISES FOR CHAPTER 3

1. (a) In the bass-clef part there are two background lines. Circle the notes that make up the bottom line. (The first note is already circled.)

   (b) Write this line in eighth notes on the blank staff below.

MENDELSSOHN: *Songs Without Words,* Op. 19, No. 2 (beginning)

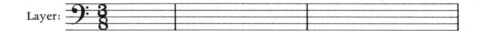

2. The following melody contains two parallel background lines. Write them on the staff below. Use only half notes and whole notes. Tie notes where necessary.

PAUL SIMON: "A Poem on the Underground Wall," mm. 45-48

3. This example shows a clear arpeggiation of three lines. Write these lines
   on the staff below. The first notes are already given.

BEETHOVEN: Sonata, Op. 81a
        (3rd movement, "Le Retour"), mm. 176-181

4. At two places in the following example a single line splits into two lines.
   At each point where this occurs circle the two notes that result.

BEETHOVEN: Sonata, Op. 31, No. 1 (3rd movement), mm. 29-31

5. Write each of the arpeggiations as block chords on the blank staff below.
   With arrows show any splitting or merging of lines (as was done in Example 5).

BEETHOVEN: Sonata, Op. 2, No. 1 (4th movement), m. 170

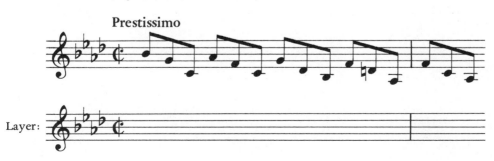

6. (a) The following example contains seven background lines. Write them on the staves indicated. The first notes in each line are given.

MENDELSSOHN: *Songs Without Words*, Op. 53, No. 3, mm. 96-99

(b) What is the relationship between the arpeggiated lines and the treble-clef lines? _____

7. In the following passage three lines are being arpeggiated. Write them on the blank staff provided.

BACH: Partita No. 3 for Unaccompanied Violin, mm. 20-22

(a) In which measure does the suspension occur?_____

(b) To what note does the suspended note resolve?_____

CHAPTER 4

PASSING MOTION

A. TERMINOLOGY

In each example so far only one "analytical layer" has been used to show the background lines.[1] However, most of our analyses from this point on will require more than one such layer. We shall refer to the individual layers in these analyses as "levels" and reserve the term "layer" for use in more general references. (For example, one might refer to the third *level* of a particular *layer* analysis). There will, of course, be situations where the distinction is not clear, and in such cases either term will do.

The number of levels necessary for the analysis of any particular passage is entirely dependent on how much information is to be conveyed on each level, what the structural relationships are, and how much detail the analysis displays. There is no minimum or maximum, but, in general, the more complex the passage the more levels will be necessary. A partial analysis, of course, may need only one.

All levels underlying a passage are considered *background* levels. However, when comparing individual levels (underlying the same passage) those closest to the passage itself are said to be relatively *foreground* while those further back, or deeper, are said to be relatively *background* (e.g., in Example 1, level 1 is relatively more foreground than level 2). The absolute foreground is the passage itself (or the complete piece), and the absolute background is the level after which no more reduction is possible. From now on all passages to be analyzed will be labeled "foreground," and the background levels numbered successively. (See Example 1.)

B. LAYER NOTATION FOR ARPEGGIATION

In the extraction of simpler analytical layers we will be dealing primarily with three types of structural relationships: *arpeggiation, passing motion,* and *neighbor motion.* In order to clearly display these relationships (within a level) each is notated in a different way.

Arpeggiation, when all its constituent notes are *members of the same chord,* is notated with white notes beamed together.[2] (See Example 1.)

---

1. In Chapter 3, for instance, there was always more than one background line on each layer, and for some examples (Example 5 and Question 6) more than one clef was necessary to display these lines. All of these analyses, however, incorporated only *one* level.

2. Arpeggiations in which all the notes are not members of the same chord will be discussed in Chapter 6.

This beaming indicates that the notes will appear on a more background level as a vertical chord; thus notes of *different* chords are beamed separately. The representation of an arpeggiation as a vertical, or block, chord shall, from this point on, be referred to as "verticalization." The following example demonstrates:

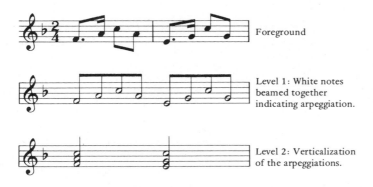

Foreground

Level 1: White notes beamed together indicating arpeggiation.

Level 2: Verticalization of the arpeggiations.

EXAMPLE 1

Neither duration nor meter is shown on levels. This makes it possible to employ beams and note values solely for the display of structural relationships. Bar lines and time signatures are omitted altogether. (Note that reducing arpeggiations to vertical chords, as on level 2 above, is similar to what you have been asked to do in previous exercises.)

C. PASSING MOTION: DEFINITION AND LAYER NOTATION

Passing motion "fills in" the distance between two other notes (i.e., an arpeggiation) by creating step motion between them. In layer notation passing *notes* are indicated by black note heads without stems, and the entire passing *motion* is spanned by a slur.

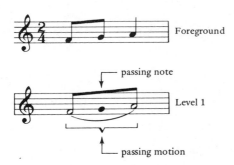

Foreground

passing note

Level 1

passing motion

EXAMPLE 2

The next level beneath a passing motion should show the passing notes deleted and only the arpeggiation remaining. See level 2 of the example below.

SMETANA: *Moldau* theme

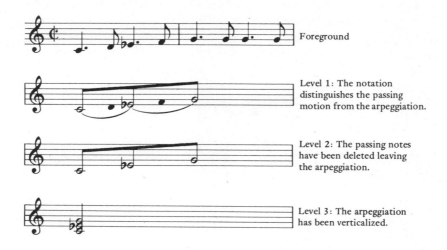

EXAMPLE 3

In Example 3 the first passing *motion* consists of C, D, and E♭, but only the D is a passing *note.* (The C and E♭ are also members of the arpeggiation and are shown as white note heads beamed together.) The second passing motion consists of E♭, F, and G, but only the F is a passing note. The span of each passing motion is marked with a slur.

Notice also in Example 3 that the rhythm of the melody (on the foreground) emphasizes the notes of the arpeggiation. If there is no such emphasis in the course of the passing motion (as in the following example), the slur should span the *entire* passing motion, and all the interim notes should be indicated with black note heads. In the first measure of the following example all of the sixteenth notes (even though some are members of the B♭ triad) are passing tones, so that the passing motion spans an octave. The same is true of the similar figure two measures later. Notice also that only the arpeggiated notes of the same chord are beamed together and that there are two chords.

MOZART: *The Magic Flute* (from an aria of the Queen of the Night)

EXAMPLE 4

In Example 4 there could have been a level between level 1 and 2 showing only the arpeggiated notes with the passing notes deleted. This was done in Examples 1 and 3. However, such an obvious level, clearly inferable from levels 1 and 2, can be omitted.

Simultaneous passing motions may be synchronized exactly with one another or simply overlap, and they may proceed at the same or different speeds. In the following example the passing motion in the treble clef moves faster and spans less time than the slower-moving passing motion in the bass clef.

BACH: *Anna Magdalena Bach Notebook,* No. 2

EXAMPLE 5

Again, notice that rhythmic emphasis and melodic contour help define the extent of the passing motion. In the next example all the passing notes are simultaneous. They are also members of the V_7 chord, but their function is that of passing notes because of their position in the phrase and lack of rhythmic emphasis.

MOZART: Sonata in F (K. 332), mm. 12-14

EXAMPLE 6

SUMMARY

Arpeggiations within the same chord are notated on levels as white notes beamed together. At a more background level these notes will be shown as vertical sonorities.

Passing notes fill in the distance between two different notes (usually arpeggiations). They are notated as black note heads, and the entire passing motion is marked with a slur. Passing notes are deleted in subsequent background levels.

EXERCISES FOR CHAPTER 4

1. Analyze the following measure from a Bach organ prelude as instructed at each level, then answer questions (a) and (b).

BACH: Prelude and Fugue in G major, m. 8

Foreground

Level 1: Notate the arpeggiations with white notes. Beam them together by chord.

Level 2: Verticalize the arpeggiations.

(a) In the background line of level 2 to what note does the first bass-clef F♯ move? _____

(b) In level 2 how are the top two and bottom two lines related?_____

_____

2. Analyze as instructed on each level, then answer (a) and (b).

MOZART: Sonata in C (K. 309), mm. 35-36

Allegro con spirito

Foreground: (a) Place a bracket under each chord area. (b) There are only two passing notes in this example; circle each.

Level 1: This level shows only the arpeggiation of the right-hand part. Add the passing notes in the appropriate notation.

Level 2: Reduce the entire passage to two vertical sonorities.

(a) In the background lines of level 2, to what note does the bass note G (in the first chord) move? _____

(b) In level 2, to what note does the treble note G (in the first chord) move? _____

3. Reduce the following passage as instructed on each level, then answer a)
   and b).

MOZART: Sonata in F for Piano, Four Hands (K. 497)
        (1st movement, primo piano), mm. 197-199

Foreground: Circle
every passing note.

Level 1: Add the
passing notes using
the correct notation.

Level 2: Show the
arpeggiations as
vertical sonorities.

(a) In level 2, *to* what note does the first F move? _____

(b) In level 2, *from* what note does the last F come? _____

4. Analyze as instructed on each level.

HANDEL: Suite No. 1 (Allemande), mm. 17-19

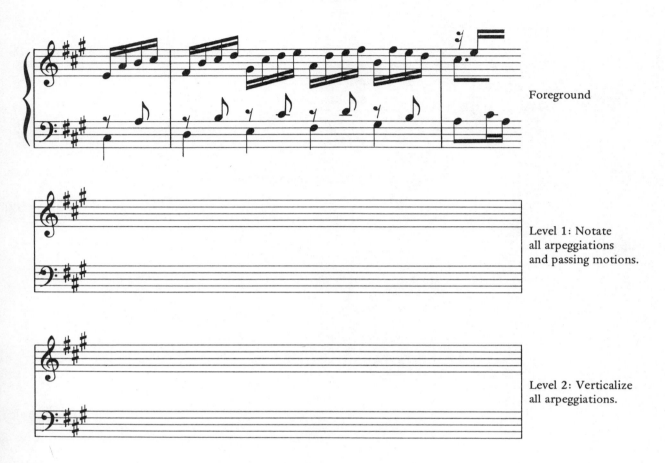

Foreground

Level 1: Notate all arpeggiations and passing motions.

Level 2: Verticalize all arpeggiations.

(a) In level 2, to what note does the bass-clef D in the fourth verticalization go? _____

(b) What grounds would one have for claiming that there was a sense in which that same D (in level 2) was present in the fifth verticalization?

_____

CHAPTER 5

NEIGHBOR MOTION

A. DEFINITION AND LAYER NOTATION

Neighbor motion is a three-note configuration in the form: *first note — neighbor note —* and return to *first note.* The neighbor note may be either upper or lower as is shown in the following foreground examples:

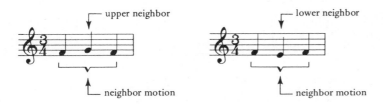

EXAMPLE 1

The neighbor may be a half step or a whole step away from the first note. (Any larger interval would turn such a configuration into an arpeggiation.)

The following example shows the layer notation for neighbor motion:

EXAMPLE 2

The first and last notes are notated as white notes, while the neighbor is a black note. *All* the notes are stemmed and beamed together, and the entire neighbor motion is marked with a slur. (Compare this with the layer notation for passing motion.)

As with passing motion the black note head will be deleted on the next level, and eventually the beamed-together white notes (on a still further background level) will be combined to form a single configuration. In the case of neighbor motion this resulting configuration is only a single note (rather than two notes which result from the reduction of passing motion). The following example illustrates:

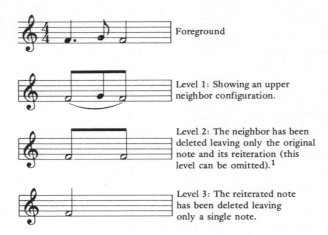

Foreground

Level 1: Showing an upper neighbor configuration.

Level 2: The neighbor has been deleted leaving only the original note and its reiteration (this level can be omitted).[1]

Level 3: The reiterated note has been deleted leaving only a single note.

EXAMPLE 3

As with passing motion, neighbor motion may be included within the notation of longer arpeggiations. For example:

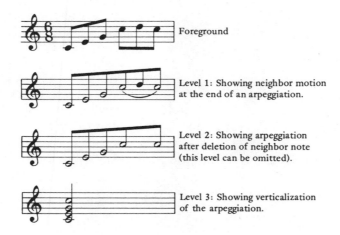

Foreground

Level 1: Showing neighbor motion at the end of an arpeggiation.

Level 2: Showing arpeggiation after deletion of neighbor note (this level can be omitted).

Level 3: Showing verticalization of the arpeggiation.

EXAMPLE 4

Notice in the above example that the reduction of the neighbor motion to a *single* note occurred on the same level as the verticalization of the arpeggiation. We will consider these two operations analogous and use "verticalization" to mean not only "block chord" display of arpeggiations but single-note reductions of neighbor motions.

B. NEIGHBOR MOTION IN CONTEXT

There are many examples in context where the neighbor note does not change the harmonic support of the passage. That is, the first note of the neighbor configuration is a member of the supporting chord but the actual

---

1. Layers such as the second level in Example 3 and Example 4 may be omitted since the relationships between the levels on either side (1 and 3) are clear without them.

neighbor note isn't. This makes the neighbor note a dissonance (reinforcing the view that we hear neighbor notes as elaborations of a one-note background figure). The following example demonstrates:

SULLIVAN: *H. M. S. Pinafore,* "We Sail the Ocean Blue"

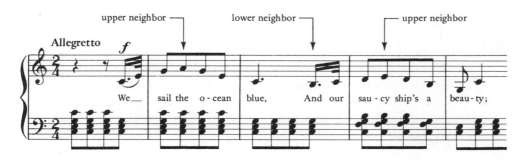

EXAMPLE 5

In the case of *each* neighbor note above observe that the harmony does not change, and the neighbor notes are therefore dissonant with the chords being repeated. (The chord in the fourth measure is a V_7 with a pedal C in the bass.)

In the following melody the neighbor notes are easily distinguishable from the arpeggiation. For instance, in the first measure all the D's receive rhythmic emphasis, and all skips outline the D-minor triad. The adjacent step motion—D, C♯, D—is clearly neighbor motion. A parallel situation occurs in the second measure.

BACH: *Six Little Preludes,* No. 3

EXAMPLE 6

After the two arpeggiations have been verticalized in level 2, note that three lines have been revealed. These are marked with arrows.

In the above example a level showing only the arpeggiation was omitted. Such a level could have gone between the present level 1 and level 2. It would have appeared as follows:

EXAMPLE 7

Examples 3 and 4 included such a level, but *every* level need not be shown in an analysis so long as the relationships are clear between the levels that *are* shown.

The following example[2] shows two parallel neighbor motions (in the left-hand part) behind a foreground of arpeggiation. Since the neighbors are exactly parallel they are stemmed together. Note that the direction of the stemming is reversed for the second set of parallel neighbors in order to clearly distinguish them from the first set.

MOZART: Sonata in F (K. 280)
      (3rd movement) mm. 42-46

Foreground

Level 1: Showing two sets of parallel neighbor motions in the lower lines.

EXAMPLE 8

C. STRUCTURAL HIERARCHIES

When one reduces a foreground or level to a simpler level one is, in addition to displaying the underlying counterpoint, representing relative structural hierarchies. The deeper the level on which a figure appears, the greater its structural importance. In Example 3 the fact that only the F remains by the third level is a way of demonstrating that F is structurally the most important entity of that configuration.

The same applies to passing motion. Passing notes are deleted at a relatively early level of analytical reduction, leaving the arpeggiation visable at a deeper level. Of course, the remaining arpeggiation may be verticalized on a

---

2. The reason for beaming together the arpeggiations of the treble-clef lines in cases such as this (level 2) will be discussed in Chapter 7.

still deeper level and subject to further analysis reductions. As this reduction process continues, relatively less important structural elements continue to be deleted until no more reductions are possible.

An obvious (and correct) conclusion to be made from the notation and reduction procedures of passing motion and neighbor motion is that there is a sense in which passing notes and neighbor notes are structurally inferior to the notes from which they arise. (Neighbor notes arise from one note, while passing notes require two, i.e., an arpeggiation.) Hierarchization of this kind is an important characteristic of layer analysis. Certainly we do not hear all the notes in a musical passage as equal; thus the representation of hierarchization is important in the analysis of music written within this system.

It should be pointed out that reference to a note on a level that is several levels removed from the foreground is not necessarily a reference to a *specific* note on the foreground. In the earlier references to the F on level 3 of Example 3 we were not referring to the F that occurs on the first beat (of the foreground) or the F that occurs on the third beat, but to the F on the third level which, on that level, encompasses both foreground F's as well as the neighboring G. (See Example 3.) Thus the F of level 3 is a symbol for a foreground configuration, not a particular member of that configuration.

SUMMARY

Neighbor motion (both upper and lower) comes in the form: *first note — neighbor note —* and *first note.* In levels, neighbor motion is notated similarly to passing motion except a neighbor note has a stem, while a passing note does not.

layer notation
for neighbor motion

layer notation
for passing motion

EXAMPLE 9

On a subsequent level the neighbor note is deleted and the entire configuration represented by a single note.

Configurations that appear on relatively background levels are structurally more important than configurations that appear on relatively foreground levels.

Some levels may be omitted within an analysis as long as the relationships are clear between the levels that are shown.

EXERCISES FOR CHAPTER 5

1. Analyze the following melody as instructed at each level.

Foreground: Place a bracket underneath each chord area (there are only four) and circle each neighbor note.

Level 1: This level shows only the arpeggiations. Add the neighbor notes using the correct notation.

Level 2: Reduce the entire passage to four vertical sonorities, then add arrows to show the background lines (as was done in Example 5 of this chapter).

BACH: Suite No. 1 for Cello (Prelude)

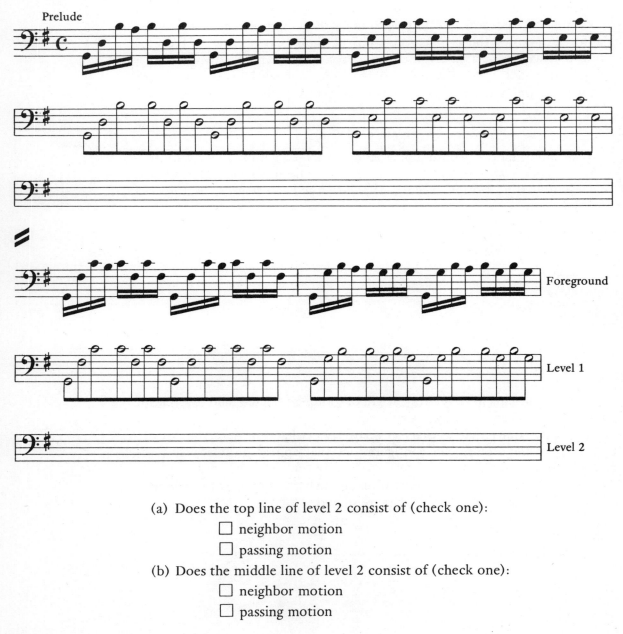

(a) Does the top line of level 2 consist of (check one):

☐ neighbor motion

☐ passing motion

(b) Does the middle line of level 2 consist of (check one):

☐ neighbor motion

☐ passing motion

(c) If there were another level below level 2 it would consist of a single chord. The chord would be (check one):

☐ C major

☐ G major

☐ D major

2. Analyze the following passage as instructed.

(a) The treble-clef line of level 1 gives only some of the arpeggiated notes. Add all the remaining notes from the foreground using the correct notation.

(b) Write out the bass-clef part of the analysis in its entirety. The beaming in the treble-clef part is to distinguish the two phrases; preserve this same beaming in the bass-clef part.

(c) The entire passage could be reduced to a single chord. What is that chord? _____

BACH: Two-part Inventions, No. 8

Foreground

Level 1

3. The following exercise gives the foreground and most of the second level of a four-measure fragment.

   (a) On the foreground put a bracket under each chord area and label with letter names (do not show inversions), e.g., ⌞____⌟ ⌞____⌟
   D maj.   E min.

   (b) On level 1 write in the bass-clef arpeggiations. Beam all the notes in the same chord together.

   (c) On level 1 notate the treble-clef part, correctly showing arpeggiations, neighbor notes, and passing notes. Beam the notes of the arpeggiations together by chord. The C in (foreground) measure 3 will have to be notated as an isolated passing note between two different arpeggiations.

   (d) Level 2 verticalizes the arpeggiations of level 1. The bottom two lines in the bass clef are large-scale neighbor motions. Add the two black note heads (for these neighbor notes) to the empty stem marked with an arrow.

   (e) If there were another level below level 2 it would consist of one chord.

   What would that chord be? _____

CLEMENTI: Sonatina, Op. 36, No. 3 (2nd movement)

4. The following example contains a neighbor to a note which is itself a neighbor. Analyze the passage as instructed at each level. Do not notate the upper note of the trill.

HANDEL: Suite No. 6 (Gigue)

Foreground

Write in the arpeggiations and neighbor motions using the correct notation.

Level 1

Verticalize the configurations from level 1.

Level 2

Notate the top line as neighbor motion. The lower arpeggiations are given.

Level 3

Notate the bass-clef part as two simultaneous passing motions.

(a) What note is a neighbor of a neighbor? _____

(b) If the passage were reduced one more level it would be a single configuration. What would that configuration be? _____

CHAPTER 6

WHAT IS AN ANALYSIS?

You have now been introduced to the major techniques of layer analysis, and most of the remaining chapters will deal with extensions of those techniques. Before proceeding, however, we shall attempt to gain a better perspective on the material that has been presented so far by considering a sample analysis and some questions about layer analysis in general. What does a complete analysis look like, and what can we expect from it?

A. PROLONGATION AND REDUCTION

The concepts of prolongation and reduction will not be new to you. In fact, we have been dealing with both of them from the very beginning. Reduction is perhaps the more obvious since that is how we have been deriving levels. Reduction is the simplification of a foreground passage (or level) to a more fundamental level. These "simplifications," of course, do not subtract from our impression of a piece of music. They are interpretations of the specific details of a piece, and thus *add* to our overall view of the music.

Prolongation is the opposite of reduction. It is the viewing of a foreground passage (or level) as an *elaboration* of a simpler background configuration. For instance, arpeggiation is a method of prolonging a background simultaneity; neighbor motion is a method of prolonging a single (background) note, etc.

B. READING AN ANALYSIS "BOTH" WAYS

It is important that a layer analysis make sense "both" ways, depending on the order in which one examines the levels. Starting at the foreground and reading down, each successive level should be a clear reduction of the level just above it. Starting at the bottom and reading up (toward the foreground), each level should be a clear prolongation of the level just below it. Thus any level within a layer analysis must be clearly a reduction of the level just above it and a prolongation of the level just below it. In the following example if one reads down (from the specific to the general), one begins by examining the foreground. Next, examine level 1; it should be a clear reduction of the foreground. Next, level 2 should be a clear reduction of level 1, and so forth. Reading up (from the general to the specific), level 2 should be a clear prolongation of level 3, and level 1 a prolongation of level 2. The same relationships hold for non-adjacent levels. For example, foregrounds are prolongations of *all* the layers which underlie them.

MOZART: Sonata in C for Piano, Four Hands (K. 521)
(1st movement, secondo piano), mm. 42-44

EXAMPLE 1

C. PROLONGATION IN PARTICULAR

Arpeggiation, passing motion, and neighbor motion are the primary agents of prolongation and are called the prolongation operators. While there are other analytical procedures used in layer analysis, most are extensions of these three operators.

Prolongation has nothing to do with making a note or passage longer. A configuration on a level has no duration at all except through its association with the foreground passage that it represents. Thus, practically speaking, every level is the same duration as the level (or foreground) that it underlies.

Prolongations are understood in terms of the simpler configurations which underlie them. A prolongation, in its most basic sense, can be described as something relatively complex which serves as an elaboration of something that is relatively simple (assuming certain relationships between the two). Prolongation, therefore, implies the existence of at least two levels, and, of course, in most analyses there are many, many more.

It is important to realize that prolongation is not an attempt to create (or re-create) a compositional process.[1] Prolongation is an aspect of analysis. While it represents the way we understand a passage (and thus is related both to composition and to analysis), the difference between it and composition is the difference between a theory that accounts for a phenomenon and the process by which that phenomenon is created.

D. DIFFERENCES AMONG THE OPERATORS

Arpeggiation is different from the other two prolongation operators in that it doesn't generate new notes. Every arpeggiated note is a note that was the result of either passing motion or neighbor motion in a (relatively) more background layer. There is a sense in which *all* notes are first "created" through neighbor motion and passing motion, and then "realized" by arpeggiation. One can think of them as being "performed" by the arpeggiation operation.

Neighbor motion is different from passing motion in that it is the prolongation of only one note and can generate only one note, while passing motion prolongs two notes and generates one or more notes between them. All the members of a neighbor motion are members of the same line. All the members of a passing motion are also members of the same line *on that level.* However, the two outer members of a passing motion are members of *two different lines on a deeper background level.* (For example, see the passing motion in the third measure in Example 2.)

E. A SAMPLE ANALYSIS

As was stated in the first chapter, a layer analysis is a way of displaying the total contrapuntal fabric of a piece of music. What may not have been clear at that point was that the lines of this contrapuntal fabric exist on many different levels of generality. As one arrives at simpler and simpler levels (i.e., levels further in the background), the lines represent larger and larger spans of time. Eventually the lines displayed will span the entire length of the composition. Consider the following analysis. Level 1 shows a brief initial line consisting of a passing motion from G up to C. This line is totally contained within the C arpeggiation and therefore subsumed into the verticalization on level 2. The verticalization of the arpeggiations of level 2 reveals deeper lines (displayed on level 3) which span the entire length of the seg-

---

1. It is easy to see why there has been a certain amount of confusion over prolongation. While it is perfectly easy to speak of "reducing" a passage of music to simpler configurations in the process of an analysis, and having a name for that process, it is another matter to speak of an actual passage of music as being an elaboration of a hypothetical construct which exists only by virtue of that analysis. However, it is this "reversal" of reduction (i.e., prolongation) which provides the necessary "generative" aspect to the theory behind layer analysis. An adequate understanding of any phenomenon, which comes about through a complete (or adequate) theory of that phenomenon, requires that such a theory predict entirely (thereby accounting for) all possible examples or occurrences of that phenomenon. Thus it is theoretically possible for an adequate analytical theory to account for all tonal composition in existence and all tonal compositions that may exist in the future. Those compositions it cannot account for, assuming the theory to be adequate, are by definition not tonal.

It should be added that there exists no entirely adequate theory of tonal music (just as there is no entirely adequate theory of any natural language). Some of the major shortcomings of the theory on which layer analysis is based will be discussed in the last chapter.

ment. When this is verticalized a single triad results, level 4, which is the furthest possible background level.

Observe on level 3 that several notes, all G's (which were present on level 2), have been deleted as a notational convenience. These notes constitute two less important lines (neither moves) and are deleted on level 3 to make room for notation of more important lines.

FRIEDLAW: Sonata No. 1

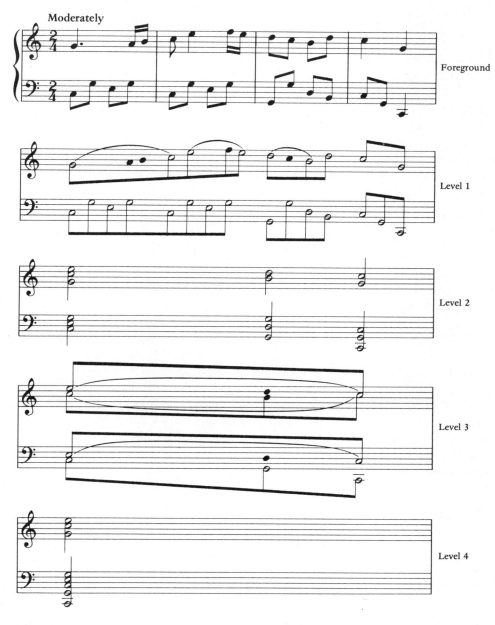

EXAMPLE 2

Of course, a foreground of only four measures would not usually constitute an entire composition. We can consider the foreground in Example 2 a complete segment, however, because it reduces to a background level of one chord and because it displays the essential I—V—I motion in the bass.[2] Because of the length and space required for the analysis of an entire composition in layer analysis, the longest examples in this book are complete segments only. Complete segments are simply passages which reduce to a single triad and which are spanned by a I—V—I bass arpeggiation. (The bass arpeggiation is, of course, one level higher than the level on which the single triad appears.) The analysis of complete segments is in most respects the same as the analysis of complete pieces.

It is thus that an efficient tonal analysis enables one to conceptualize a tonal composition as a *prolongation of a single triad.* And that triad, not surprisingly, is the tonic triad of the piece.

An analysis should show that every note in a composition has a network of relationships that relates it to the other notes of its immediate context. The notes within this context are, in turn, related to larger configurations, and these to larger, and so forth until the most general level is reached: the level containing only the single triad.

There must be several strong cautions made at this point. First of all, the triad about which we are speaking, the one that constitutes the furthest background level, is not a specific group of notes somewhere in the piece. It is a symbol representing the entire piece. Do not look for a tonic triad within a composition to call *the* background triad.

Further, this triad should not be thought of as an "answer" or solution to the analysis. Since every tonal composition is a prolongation of a single triad, it is hardly significant for an analysis to yield a triad on the last level. It is the relationships displayed on the levels and the relationships between these levels that tell one about the structure of the piece; these are the most significant parts of the analysis.

SUMMARY

Through layer analysis a tonal composition is viewed as a prolongation of a single triad. The three primary prolongation operators are passing motion, neighbor motion, and arpeggiation, and it is by the repeated application of these operators that successively more complex layers are generated until the foreground is reached.

In making a layer analysis it is not arriving at a single triad at the most background level that is important, but rather the proper display of the contrapuntal lines that lie between the foreground and the furthest background level, and the relationships of these lines to one another.

Among the operators only passing motion and neighbor motion generate notes. Arpeggiation simply articulates notes that have already been generated.

---

2. This particular bass arpeggiation will be discussed in Chapter 9.

CHAPTER 7

LAYER NOTATION

A. THE PURPOSE OF LAYER NOTATION

The notational devices of layer analysis make it possible to (1) indicate the function of each note, (2) indicate relative structural hierarchies, and (3) differentiate background lines. These are important aspects of analysis, and we shall consider each in more detail.

1. INDICATE THE FUNCTION OF EACH NOTE

Through the layer notation demonstrated in the previous chapters one can indicate whether a note is a passing note, a neighbor note, or part of an arpeggiation. A clear and immediately recognizable specification of these functions is particularly important since (for the same note) they will often change from level to level. In the following example consider the first note, an E. On level 1 the notation indicates that it is a note of an arpeggiated figure. On level 2 it is the first note of a neighbor motion, and on level 3 it is the first note of a passing motion.

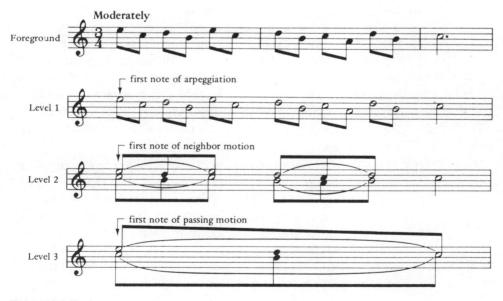

EXAMPLE 1

Notice in Example 1 that each of the different functions (in which the E is notated) spans a different amount of time. On level 1 the arpeggiation encompasses only the first two notes. The neighbor motion on level 2 encompasses the first six (foreground) notes, and the passing motion of level 3 spans the entire passage.

That a note is capable of serving in different capacities simultaneously is an indication of the richness of the tonal system. While it might be thought that such multiple functions (albeit on different levels) would add an undesirable degree of ambiguity, they, in fact, add additional interest to the music which they underlie.

2. INDICATION OF RELATIVE STRUCTURAL HIERARCHIES

Relative structural hierarchies are indicated by a combination of levels and layer notation. You have already seen in Chapter 5, Section B, how levels are used to indicate relative structural hierarchies. The deeper the level on which a configuration appears, the greater its structural importance. In a more restricted sense the notation within each level shows this also. White notes, for instance, are of greater structural importance than black notes. In general, however, the notation is used to show finer structural differentiations than those shown by levels.

3. DIFFERENTIATION OF BACKGROUND LINES

Before discussing the differentiation of background lines it should be pointed out that it takes at least three notes to complete a passing motion or neighbor motion. However, we will often be referring to excerpts in which there are only two notes present in a line, and sometimes only one. It is to be understood in such a situation that the example being considered is incomplete, and that there are other notes in the remainder of the piece that will complete these lines.[1]

(a) Notation for passing motion and neighbor motion groups notes which are in the same relative background line. All the members of the same passing motion are members of the same line (although they will be members of different lines on a deeper level), and all the members of the same neighbor motion are members of the same line. Thus the notation, which shows the passing or neighbor relationship between specific notes, helps sort out the notes of a foreground into their respective background lines.

(b) The situation with respect to the notation of arpeggiation and its relationship to lines is more complicated than is the case with passing motion and neighbor motion as described above. The initial instructions for the notation of arpeggiation (Chapter 4) stated that only notes within the same chord were to be beamed together. There is, from this initial instruction, a danger that one would think that the notation of arpeggiation is for the purpose of distinguishing chords. It is not, and now that we have been exposed to more complex background lines the purpose of arpeggiation notation must be clarified and the instructions for its application modified.

1. An exception is a line which does not move (i.e., which *does* consist of one note). Such a line is relatively insignificant and is usually deleted. See also the section on incomplete neighbor motion in the next chapter.

B. DIFFERENTIATION OF BACKGROUND LINES THROUGH ARPEGGIATION NOTATION

The notation of arpeggiation is not for the purpose of distinguishing chords, nor is it solely for distinguishing arpeggiation. It is for differentiating background lines. To do this efficiently the criteria for notating arpeggiation must be modified in the following way: do not beam together any notes such that, when verticalized, will yield more pitches than background lines.

For example, the following passage is obviously made up of arpeggiations, but to attempt to show all the notes as members of the *same* arpeggiation (i.e., beam them together) would violate the above instruction. When verticalized such an arpeggiation would yield the incorrect results on level 2 indicating the presence of six different background lines.

EXAMPLE 2

Beaming the arpeggiations so that there are never more notes in one arpeggiation than there are background lines yields the following analysis of the same foreground (clearly displaying the underlying passing and neighbor motion).

EXAMPLE 3

While it is fairly clear from the foreground of the preceding example that there are only two lines present, there will be more complex examples where the number of background lines will not be immediately apparent. In analyzing a passage do not expect to be able to see all the background lines immediately. You will thus not be able to proceed "cleanly" from level to level, finishing one completely before proceeding to the next. It will often be that an entire level must be written out before one can see that it is incorrect. For an efficient analysis technique, one must be willing to skip back and forth between levels, to revise former levels, and, in short, to work on all levels at once.

In the example above, levels 1, 2, and 4 are not absolutely necessary. Level 3 clearly shows the underlying counterpoint, and the connections between it and the foreground are clear. In general, the display of background lines is the essential part of a layer analysis. However, additional levels can be included at the discretion of the analyst if they help to clarify or differentiate these lines.

Notice, again, that repeated notes *can* be beamed together (even if there are intervening notes) if they can be represented in the verticalization on a subsequent level as a single note. They would thus be considered reiterations of one pitch of a background line. (See the sixth example in Chapter 5 for an example.)

C. DETERMINING THE BACKGROUND LINES

In order to determine the correct background lines (and thus assign to the pitches their relative contrapuntal functions), one must take into consideration aspects of both pitch and rhythm. Most strings of notes, without rhythmic differentiation or other simultaneous pitches, could have more than one interpretation. For example:

EXAMPLE 4

Rhythmless and without accompanying pitches, it could be interpreted in many ways. The *Moldau* theme (quoted in Chapter 4) which employs those same pitches makes clear, through rhythmic emphasis, that a C-minor triad is being arpeggiated:

SMETANA: *Moldau* theme

EXAMPLE 5

Even without other simultaneously sounding pitches the above example is clear. However, the same notes in a *different* rhythmic setting could yield a different interpretation. The following figure would seem to arpeggiate from D to G:

EXAMPLE 6

The next example was used in Chapter 4 as a clear case of passing motion. Notice particularly the notes in the treble clef.

BACH: *Anna Magdalena Bach Notebook, No. 2*

EXAMPLE 7

The same treble-clef notes appear in the following example but they are articulated with different rhythms, and, further, different notes in the bass clef add support to the rhythmic changes of the top lines. (Note, it is *very* important to play Examples 5 through 8 in order to hear the differences between them.)

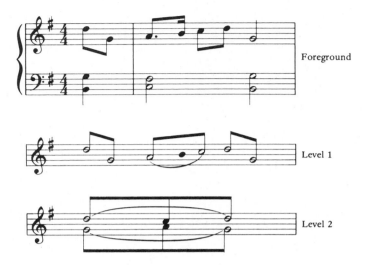

EXAMPLE 8

Since the same string of notes can have different interpretations, as demonstrated in Examples 5 through 8, decision-making with respect to assigning contrapuntal functions must take into account rhythm and relationships among other pitches present. As one would suspect, there will often be ambiguities, but a satisfactory solution can usually be reached by carefully weighing these two factors.

SUMMARY

Layer analysis notation enables one to:

    (1) indicate the function of each note;
    (2) indicate structural hierarchies;
    (3) differentiate background lines.

In notating arpeggiations, do not beam any notes together that when verticalized will yield more pitches than there are background lines. This aids in the differentiation of these lines.

In determining background lines one must consider rhythmic emphasis as well as the relationships between all notes within the context under consideration.

EXERCISES FOR CHAPTER 7

1. Analyze this fragment as directed for each level.

  Level 1: Show only arpeggiations. Each will contain two notes.

  Level 2: Verticalize the arpeggiations.

  Level 3: Notate the neighbor motions. The sustained line is already given.

  Level 4: Delete the neighbor motions and notate a passing motion.

MOZART: Sonata in F (K. 332)
      (3rd movement), mm. 3-4

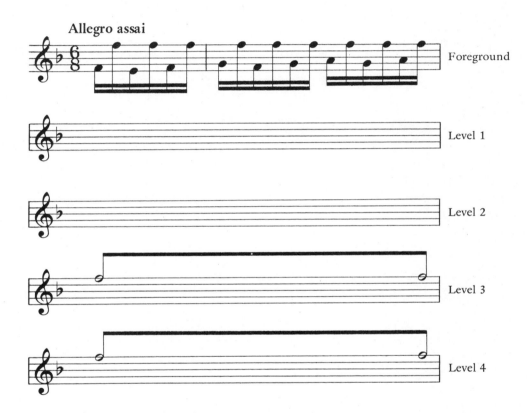

2. Analyze only the bass-clef part on each level as instructed.

Level 1: Notate the arpeggiations.

Level 2: Verticalize the arpeggiations.

Level 3: Two bass-clef staves are given on which to indicate the background lines (of the bass-clef part). Notate the bottom two lines on the bottom staff and the top two on the top staff.

BEETHOVEN: Bagatelles, Op. 119, No. 3, mm. 42-45

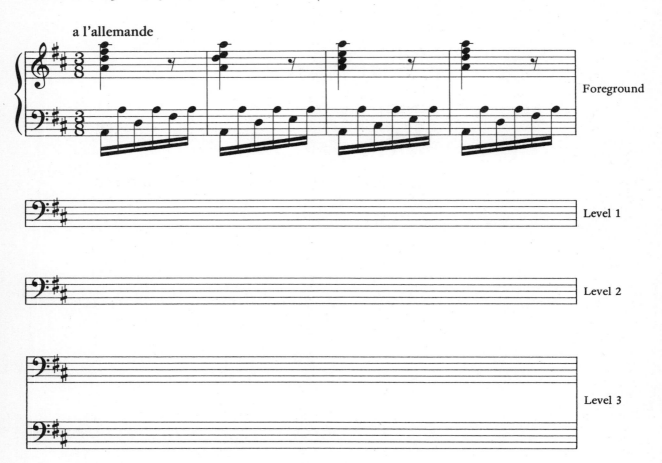

3. Analyze as directed for each level.

Level 1: Notate the arpeggiations.

Level 2: Verticalize the arpeggiations.

Level 3: Often the background lines of upper parts are more complex than the background lines underlying lower parts. In this example the treble-clef parts require one more level of reduction than the bass-clef parts. On this level show only the treble-clef parts. Notate *only* two background lines. The top should consist of a string of neighbor motions, the bottom a passing motion. All other notes may be deleted.

Level 4: The bass line is given. Notate the remaining three moving lines that span this example.

BEETHOVEN: Variations on "Nel cor più non mi sento" (var. 6)

CHAPTER 8

ADDITIONAL TYPES OF PASSING
AND NEIGHBOR MOTION

A. CHROMATIC PASSING MOTION

The type of passing motion we have considered thus far employs only diatonic pitches (i.e., pitches within the scale of the key). Any passing notes that are outside the key of the passage are called chromatic passing notes. On layers they are notated in the same manner as their diatonic counterparts. In the following example both passing motions contain a chromatic passing note (B♭ in the first and G♯ in the second) as well as diatonic passing notes.

BEETHOVEN: Variations on "Nel cor più non mi sento (var. 5)

Foreground

Level 1: Showing two passing motions each of which contains one chromatic passing note.

EXAMPLE 1

Within the passing motion on the foreground of the example above, the third of each chord falls on a relatively strong beat. In light of this the following is also an acceptable way of notating the passage:

EXAMPLE 2

When chromatic pitches appear in relative isolation (i.e., not as members of adjacent foreground passing notes as in Example 1), they usually indicate the presence of a strong underlying background line. In the following example the octave A naturals are a part of a chromatic passing motion that extends from the downbeat of the first measure to the downbeat of the next. (In the layer only the bass-clef part is shown.)

JOPLIN: *Maple Leaf Rag*

Foreground

Level 1 of bass-clef part showing chromatic passing notes.

EXAMPLE 3

B. PASSING MOTION BETWEEN MEMBERS OF DIFFERENT ARPEGGIATIONS

When passing notes occur between notes which are not members of the same arpeggiation notate them the same as before (i.e., black note head and slur). The difference will be that the two outer white notes will not be beamed together (since they are not members of the same arpeggiation). The following example illustrates:

Foreground

Level 1

EXAMPLE 4

See also Example 3. The octave A naturals in the bass are an example of this type of passing motion.

C. CHROMATIC NEIGHBOR NOTES

As with chromatic passing tones, chromatic neighbors are notated exactly like their diatonic counterparts. The following shows two parallel chromatic neighbors:

GOTTSCHALK: *Tournament Galop*, mm. 23-24

Foreground

Level 1: Showing two chromatic neighbor motions.

EXAMPLE 5

D. INCOMPLETE NEIGHBOR MOTION

Incomplete neighbor motions are similar to ordinary neighbor motions except the first note of the configuration is missing. We shall notate them as follows:

incomplete upper neighbor   incomplete lower neighbor

EXAMPLE 6

The following example shows incomplete neighbor notes in context:

MOZART: Sonata in A major (K. 331)
  (3rd movement, "Rondo alla Turca")

Foreground

Level 1:
Showing
incomplete
neighbor
motions.

Level 2

Level 3

EXAMPLE 7

There are seldom incomplete neighbors in context where some earlier note cannot be found to "complete" the configuration. In this example the second and third incomplete neighbors are preceded by notes (a C and E, respectively) which *could* give one grounds for considering them complete neighbors. The analysis above was decided upon because each of the sixteenth-note figures seems to be relatively self-contained, and, furthermore, since the first figure *has* to be an incomplete neighbor (it is the beginning of the piece), the remaining figures may be heard as analogous to the first.

There is another interesting feature of the incomplete neighbors of Example 7. Consider the first sixteenth-note figure. The contour and rhythm would tend to make one interpret the notes as forming passing motion:

EXAMPLE 8

However, outweighing these factors are (1) the unrelenting A-minor chord in the left hand, (2) the overall A-minor arpeggiation of the entire right-hand passage (as shown in the second level), and (3) the leap of a third across the first and second bar lines. Thus the rhythm and contour of the sixteenths is pitted against the three considerations just mentioned. Simultaneous existence of evidence to support conflicting interpretations within the same passage, even in such an apparently simple passage, adds a dimension of interest often not present in the works of lesser composers. Compare, for instance, this example with the passage by Clementi in the third exercise in Chapter 5.

Occasionally, incomplete neighbor motions appear in which the last note is missing instead of the first. Known by some as "hanging tones" or "escape tones," they are more problematic than the others and are not treated in this text. Their notation would, obviously, be the reverse of that in Example 6.

E. DOUBLE NEIGHBOR MOTION

Another type of neighbor that is sometimes found is the double neighbor. It appears in the following pattern:

EXAMPLE 9

It is actually the result of the arpeggiation of two simultaneous neighbor motions:

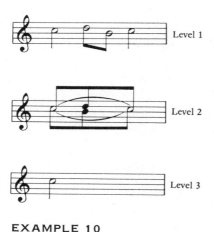

EXAMPLE 10

But we will notate it as neighbor motion in the following manner:

EXAMPLE 11

The following is a well-known example of double neighbor motion:

MOZART: *Magic Flute,* "Alles Fühlt"

EXAMPLE 12

SUMMARY

Chromatic neighbor motions and chromatic passing motions are notated the same as diatonic neighbor and passing motions.

An incomplete neighbor is a neighbor motion that is missing the initial note. It is notated:

EXAMPLE 13

A double neighbor motion is a combination of two neighbor motions and is notated as follows:

EXAMPLE 14

EXERCISES FOR CHAPTER 8

1. Complete the notation of the top background line in level 1. Notice that the last C♯ in measure one receives no rhythmic emphasis and is thus not notated as a part of the arpeggiation. There is one incomplete neighbor.

SCARLATTI: Sonata No. 23 (Longo 238), mm. 1-3

Foreground

Level 1

2. In the following example some of the arpeggiation is given in level 1. Add all of the remaining notes (including arpeggiations) using the correct notation.

JOPLIN: *A Breeze from Alabama*, mm. 5-6

Foreground

Level 1

3. In the following example the complete bass part is given on level 1. Within it there are two E's (marked with arrows) that could be mistaken for incomplete neighbor notes. Notice that they are shown on the level to be *complete* neighbors, although in each case the initial note of the neighbor motion is not immediately adjacent to the remainder of the configuration.

There are, however, two genuine incomplete neighbors in the treble-clef part. On level 1 the stationary line (on middle C) is already given. Add the remaining notes of the treble-clef part in the correct notation.

TELEMANN: Fantasia No. 2

4. On level 1 notate only the treble-clef part of the following example.

HANDEL: Passacaglia

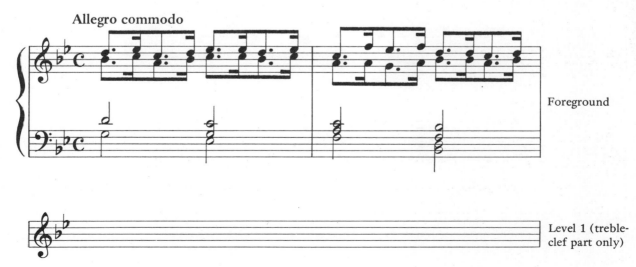

5. Notate completely level 1 of the following passage. There is one chromatic passing note, one chromatic neighbor note, and one incomplete neighbor. The treble-clef notation should show the arpeggiation of a B♭ chord in the first (foreground) measure and an F$^6_5$ chord in the second (foreground) measure.

MOZART: Piano Sonata in B♭ (K. 570) (3rd movement)

Foreground

Level 1

In the second measure of the above example an incomplete neighbor interrupts a passing motion. What is the passing *note* of that motion?_____

6. Analyze only the treble-clef part on the level provided.

FRIEDLAW: Sonata No. 2

Foreground

Level 1

With the exception of the last note, the melody of this example contains exactly the same notes as the Clementi example, the third exercise in Chapter 5. How does the background of the treble-clef part differ from that of the Clementi example? What specific events in *this* example caused those differences? _____

_____

CHAPTER 9

BASS ARPEGGIATION

There is one exception to the principle, mentioned earlier, that background lines move by step: bass lines may move by leap. Furthermore, there is one leap pattern that is structurally more important to the bass line (and musical phrases in general) than other leaps, and that is the leap from the tonic to the dominant and back: I—V—I. This pattern (or an abbreviated version, I—V) will span entire phrases and appear on a deeper level than any other bass movement. We shall refer to this pattern as the *structural bass arpeggiation* and to the dominant within it as the *structural dominant.*

In the following example every note can be accounted for as a member of some background linear step motion except the lowest D. On the third staff of level 2 the D is notated as part of an arpeggiated bass line. On the staff above observe that the first G also serves as the first note of a neighbor motion. The two G's are joined by a brace to show that they are the same note.

BEETHOVEN: Variations on "Nel cor più non mi sento" (beginning)

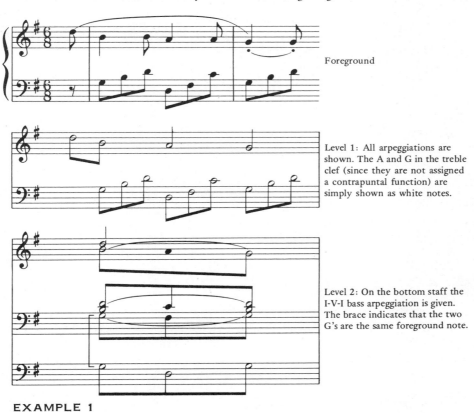

Foreground

Level 1: All arpeggiations are shown. The A and G in the treble clef (since they are not assigned a contrapuntal function) are simply shown as white notes.

Level 2: On the bottom staff the I-V-I bass arpeggiation is given. The brace indicates that the two G's are the same foreground note.

EXAMPLE 1

Example 1 was not reduced down to one chord (on a subsequent level) because when the structural bass arpeggiation is reached there is usually no reason to reduce a passage further. The background lines which those notes support are usually the most basic lines of the passage. Should one, for some reason, wish to reduce level 2 one more level (i.e., to a vertical sonority), the dominant, D, would *not* appear on the bottom despite the fact that it is the lowest note in the passage. In many cases of reduction, the root of the chord, if it appears in the bass, will take precedence over other members of the chord that might be lower. Such notes, being structurally inferior to the root, will be reduced out on a subsequent level, leaving the root as the lowest pitch.

Thus there are two differences between the bass line and the other background lines:

(1) a leap does not indicate the presence of two background lines (since the bass line itself can move by leap), and

(2) arpeggiations do not always verticalize (as in the case of the dominant in Example 1).

The following example shows a slightly more complex version of the I−V−I bass arpeggiation, this time partially filled in with passing motion. Notice that the initial passing motion in the bass goes down only to F♯ so that the structural dominant (D) can only be accounted for by arpeggiation.

BEETHOVEN: Sonata, Op. 49, No. 1, mm. 1-3

Foreground

Level 1

Level 2: Passing notes and neighbors from level 1 are deleted.

Level 3: The I-V-I bass arpeggiation underlies neighbor motion in three upper lines.

EXAMPLE 2

The bass line of the following example shows the I—V leap to the structural dominant. The dominant is preceded by an incomplete lower neighbor (which is a typical occurrence in the bass). On level 2 the neighbor is deleted, leaving only the I—V motion. Only the bass line is shown on the levels.

BEETHOVEN: Sonata Op. 14, No. 2 (2nd movement)

Foreground

Level 1: Showing only the bass. Note the incomplete neighbor to the dominant.

Level 2: Showing the bass arpeggiation.

EXAMPLE 3

SUMMARY

Bass lines may move by leap. Two patterns, I—V—I and sometimes I—V, are basic to bass lines and will appear on the deepest levels underlying a tonal passage. There is usually no need to reduce a passage further once this leap pattern, called the structural bass arpeggiation, has been reached.

EXERCISES FOR CHAPTER 9

1. The following passage is similar to Examples 1 and 2 within this chapter. Analyze as instructed for each level.

    Level 1: Show all arpeggiations (deleting any adjacent repeated notes) and neighbor and passing notes. The first configurations are given.

    Level 2: Delete the passing and neighbor notes and verticalize the arpeggiations.

    Level 3: Notate the background lines. The structural I—V—I should appear on this level. A stationary line on the E above middle C may be omitted.

HANDEL: *Seven Pieces,* No. 3, mm. 21-22

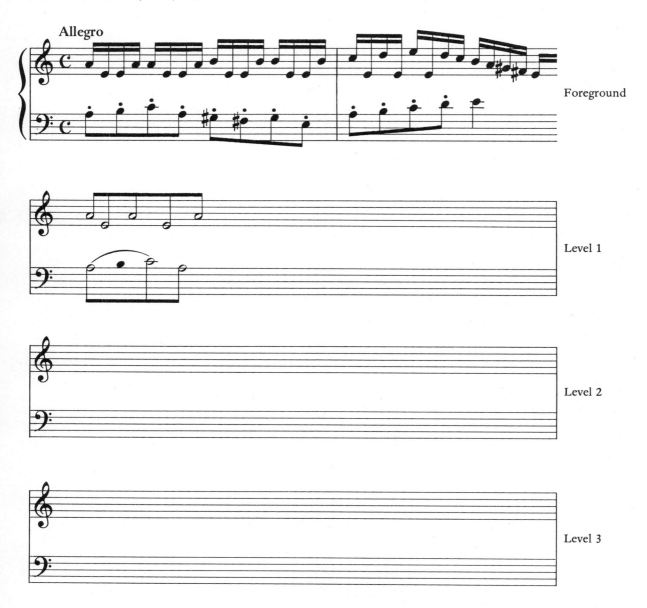

2. Analyze as instructed for each level.

Level 1: The bass notes are given. Add the upper lines. A few notes are already given. At this level the upper lines should only show arpeggiation and passing motion.

Level 2: Verticalize the arpeggiations and notate the longer-range neighbor motions and passing motions in the upper lines. The initial neighbor motions are already given.

Level 3: On the bottom staff notate the structural bass arpeggiation (with the addition of an incomplete neighbor). On the top staff notate the two background lines that span the length of the entire passage.

GOTTSCHALK: *Miserere du Trovatore*, Op. 52, mm. 33-36

What reason is there for not analyzing the first three beats of measure 2 in the following way? _____

_____

3. The following example contains a background I—V motion in the bass. Blank staves are provided for your analysis. Use two or three levels as needed. On the final level show the bass arpeggiation without neighbor notes or passing notes.

HANDEL: Suite No. 9 ("Gigue")

4. In the I—V—I bass movement any of the chords may appear in inversion. In the following example the dominant is in inversion making the structural bass line a neighbor motion (I—V$_6$—I). Analyze as instructed for each level.

Level 1: Display all arpeggiation, neighbor and passing motion.

Level 2: Verticalize all arpeggiations. In addition show the B♭ as a passing note (between two notes that are not members of the same arpeggiation).

Level 3: On the bottom staff show the bass line and the line above it (beginning on the A below middle C). On the middle staff show the line that starts on middle C. On the top staff show the top two lines.

BEETHOVEN: Sonata, Op. 2, No. 1 (Trio)

CHAPTER 10

OCTAVE EQUIVALENCE

A. TERMINOLOGY

One of the basic assumptions of tonal music is that pitches an octave apart are in a sense the "same" pitch. This assumption, called octave equivalence, is supported in part by the fact that we call such pitches by the same name. We will examine in this chapter several ways that octave equivalence affects layer analysis.

"Pitch-class" is a useful term in any discussion of octave equivalence. This term provides a convenient way of referring to all C's, all C♯'s, all D's, etc., without referring to a *specific* C, C♯, or D. We frequently use names of pitches in a pitch-class sense. For instance, we might say that the notes of a B-diminished triad are B, D, and F. We would, in such circumstances, probably not wish to list every possible B, every D, and so forth.

B. OMISSION OF OCTAVE-DOUBLED LINES

In orchestral writing the basses often double the cellos at the octave, and the second violins double the first violins at the octave; in piano writing long series of adjacent octaves are common. In none of these cases, however, are such octaves considered independent of one another. They are interpreted as a duplication or a "coloration" of what is essentially one melodic line. In a layer analysis most octaves of this type are deleted, or only those retained which are useful to the analysis.

In the following foreground there are many octave doublings, and all are deleted in level 1. To include them would clutter the level, and the essential background counterpoint is clear without them. The top line (see Example 1) is doubled at two lower octaves, and both these lower octaves have been deleted. Notice, in addition, that the bass line, for clarity, is shown at the upper of the two octaves in which it appears.

BRAHMS: Ballades, Op. 10, No. 1, mm. 14-15

EXAMPLE 1

C. OMISSION OF ISOLATED OCTAVE DOUBLINGS AND FRAGMENTARY LINES

Notes which can obviously be deleted on the first level (such as the straightforward octave doublings in Example 1) require no special notation; they can simply be omitted. However, in the analysis of more complex passages it is sometimes better to retain *all* the foreground notes in the first one or two levels and delete them after some verticalization has taken place. In this case special notation is needed.

The notation for notes that are to be deleted because of octave duplication is an x-shaped note head and an arrow indicating the note of which the note to be deleted is an octave doubling.

EXAMPLE 2

The above notation should be used on the level prior to the one in which the notes in question are actually deleted. (Example 3 illustrates.) The decision as to which note of the octave to delete depends on the rest of the passage. If one note is a part of a clear background line and the other apparently isolated, then obviously the latter should be deleted. If each note has a different contrapuntal function, then perhaps neither should be deleted.

A level-by-level explanation of Example 3 follows:

Level 1: Members of the same arpeggiated chord are beamed together. While arpeggiation notation is not for distinguishing chords (it is for distinguishing background lines), this can sometimes be a helpful first step in sorting the notes of complex passages. Notice that such a step does not violate the principle of not beaming together notes that when verticalized will yield more pitches than there are background lines. (An octave, as well as a repeated note, represents but one pitch-class.)

Level 2: The purpose of this level is to show which notes of the verticalized arpeggiations are to be omitted on the next level. (Such a level is not an *essential* part of a layer analysis.) The notes represented by x's are to be deleted, and the arrows show the notes of which they are considered octave doublings. Such notes could, of course, be left in, but they would either duplicate other movement shown or be a part of relatively unimportant lines (i.e., lines which do not move at all). Examine, for instance, the line beginning (with the x-shaped note heads) on the G below middle C. In the first, second, and fourth verticalizations *this* G remains in the same place, apparently not moving. In the third verticalization, a B-major chord, there is no G in that register nor a note a step away in either direction to which the G could have moved. An octave higher, however, a G has moved down to an F♯ in the third verticalization. The lower G is obviously part of a line that is duplicating a line an octave higher, but the lower line does not contain one of the most important members of that line (the F♯). It is obviously more efficient, then, to notate that line (which is made up solely of a neighbor motion) in the octave where it is complete and omit it in the octave where it is fragmentary.

Level 3: Three staves are used to display the lines. The top staff shows a B-octave arpeggiation filled in with passing motion. The middle staff shows two neighbor motions. Notice that the bottom neighbor motion consists of E—D—E. However, between the D and the last E, a D♯ appears as a passing note. Whether the D♯ is a chromatic passing note (D♯ *is* in the key of E minor) or whether the D natural is really a chromatic neighbor note is academic; the D♯ is a passing note—it happens to be between the second and third note of a neighbor motion. The bottom staff contains the bass arpeggiation.

CHAMINADE: *Guitare*, Op. 32 (Caprice)

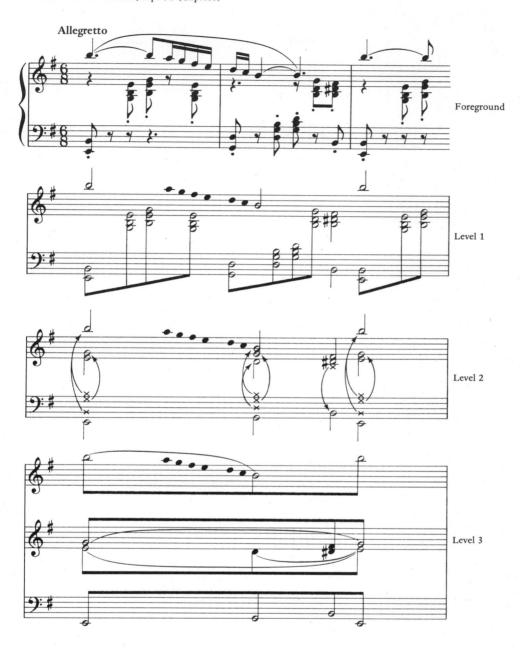

EXAMPLE 3

Let us now take another look at the foreground and the notes that were deleted because of octave equivalency. In Example 4 the passage is reprinted and all the notes to be deleted in the analysis are circled; there are eighteen in all. It can be seen from this that octave equivalence plays a major role in the deletion of notes in the reduction process.

Foreground

EXAMPLE 4

In Example 5 every verticalization shown on level 2 has one note to be deleted because of octave duplication. Reasons for the selection of notes to be deleted are given below. However, an incorrect decision will be made leading to an unsatisfactory configuration on the third level. Follow the explanation carefully.

Level 1: Verticalizations are shown.

Level 2: (a) The top part in this level is almost entirely an arpeggiation of the tonic triad (B, B, G♯, G♯, E, E). A duplication of this arpeggiation appears an octave lower (beginning on the B below middle C and continuing in every other verticalization) and, as an octave duplication, is notated with x's to be subsequently deleted.

(b) In the second verticalization the x on D♯ marks the beginning of a fragmented duplication (every other note) of the bass line and therefore is also deleted.

Level 3: The resulting configurations are displayed. In the treble clef they are an arpeggiation on top and a passing motion underneath.

At this point we come to an interesting situation concerning the top two figures in level three. On top we have a B, G♯, E arpeggiation, and underneath we have a passing motion from G♯ down to B. Which do you hear as the dominant figure in these measures? Play the passage over or listen to a recording. Which figure would be brought out in performance?

Either could be projected in performance. However, only one is a *line*, the passing motion, and it is likely that the projection[1] of a line (rather than

1. Lines may be projected in many ways (*not* just by playing the notes louder) and should be the subject of careful study in performance instruction.

an arpeggiation) would make for a more interesting performance. If the line, therefore, is to be considered the more important figure of the two it should appear on the top. Thus the earlier decision to delete the lower of the octave duplications of the arpeggiation (in the above description of level 2a) was incorrect. It was not apparent at level 2 that this was a bad decision since it is usual, given a choice, to maintain outer voices and delete inner ones. In this case, however, we arrive at an analysis that does not reflect the way we hear or think about the piece.

BEETHOVEN: Sonata, Op. 109 (1st movement)

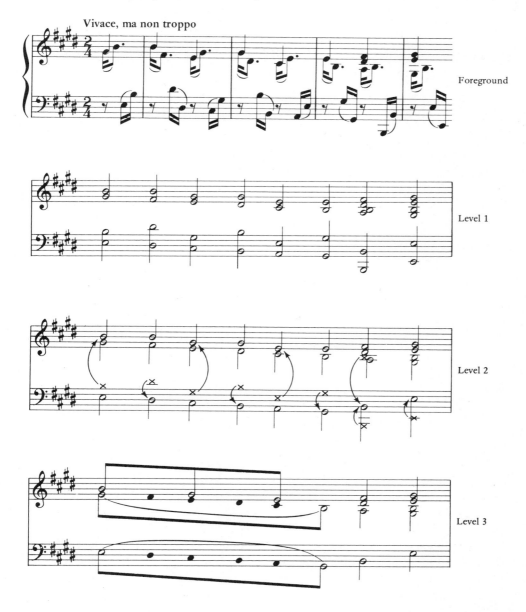

EXAMPLE 5

Example 6 gives an analysis where a different decision is made at level 2: to consider the top arpeggiation an octave transfer up from an inner voice. This leaves the descending passing motion as the top (and dominant) line in level 3.

BEETHOVEN: Sonata, Op. 109 (1st movement)

EXAMPLE 6

Level 1: Same as before.

Level 2: (a) The E, G♯, B arpeggiation in the top voice is an octave transfer up from an inner voice and as such is notated for deletion. (Repeated notes of the arpeggiation are shown tied.)

   (b) Same as before.

Level 3: The resulting configurations are displayed.

Level 4: The passing motions and arpeggiations within the tonic triad are deleted revealing neighbor motions in the treble clef, arpeggiation in the bass. In the bass clef note that the line that begins on the B below middle C splits making the A (indicated with a black note head) a combination passing note and neighbor note.

SUMMARY

Octave doublings of lines, parts of lines, or even individual notes are usually deleted on the levels. Such notes can often simply be omitted (as in Example 2). In complex passages where a notation for deletion may be helpful, use an x-shaped note head (for each note to be deleted on the next level) and draw an arrow to the note that it doubles. This notation is usually the most helpful within verticalizations.

EXAMPLE 7

EXERCISES FOR CHAPTER 10

1. On level 1 notate the lines underlying the following foreground, but in each case of a line doubled at the octave delete one line. Distribute the remaining lines among the three staves provided. (This example is simple enough that a level using the x-shaped note heads is not necessary.)

CHOPIN: Preludes, Op. 28, No. 20

2. Analyze as instructed for each level.

Level 1: Verticalize the arpeggiations. (Show the neighbors as single notes.)

Level 2: Indicate the octave duplications (within the verticalizations) with x-shaped note heads and arrows.

Level 3: Notate the four remaining background lines. Each consists of neighbor motion. (If you have more than four lines, you did not show enough octave duplications in level 2.)

CHOPIN: Preludes, Op. 28, No. 1

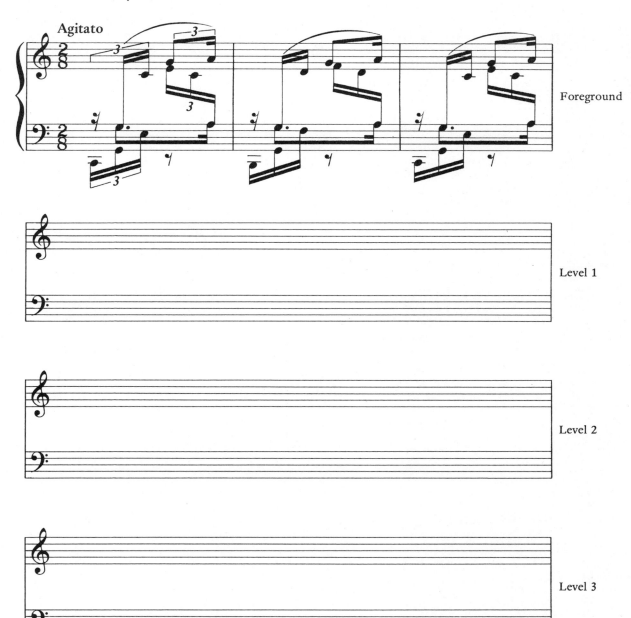

3. On each of the levels the bass-clef parts are already given. Add the treble-clef parts. In level 2 show the deletion of a fragmentary duplication of one of the descending bass-clef lines (using x-shaped note heads and arrows).

BEETHOVEN: Sonata, Op. 79 (3rd movement)

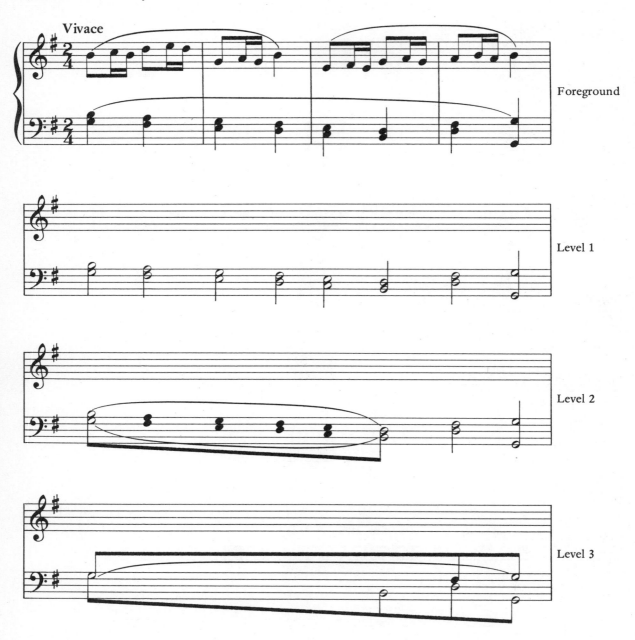

CHAPTER 11

OCTAVE TRANSFER

A. OCTAVE TRANSFER

The fact that octave duplications are so common should make it *not* surprising that background lines often skip an octave. This is not an exception to the principle that background lines usually move by step since the octave is, in a sense, the same note. This skip is called an octave transfer and is considered essentially the continuation of the same line.

In layer notation an octave transfer should be indicated by arrows as is shown in the following example.

Foreground

Level 1

EXAMPLE 1

If the octave transfers are very brief, they may be omitted altogether as in Example 2.

Foreground

Level 1

EXAMPLE 2

Sometimes octave transfers involve the leap of a seventh.

EXAMPLE 3

In the following analysis it is necessary to evoke octave transfer in order for the background lines to move by step (and for the usual suspension-resolution pattern to be displayed). Examine the third beat of measure 1. The C becomes a dissonance (a suspension) when the previous E above moves down to D. The C then resolves to a B within the fourth beat, and in the same beat a G appears above the staff while the G an octave below disappears. The upper G, last note in measure 1, is an octave transfer from the G that appears within the third beat. (See level 1.)

BACH: *Twelve Little Preludes,* No. 1

EXAMPLE 4

Aside from the fact that lines must move by step, it would not make sense contrapuntally to think of each note in the third chord as simply skipping up to the next higher note in order to account for the next chord.

EXAMPLE 5

For instance, a theoretical system within which background lines could leap in such an indiscriminate manner would make the differentiation of these lines, one from another, extremely difficult.

Apparently isolated notes which seemingly do not have a contrapuntal origin usually can be accounted for as individual octave transfers. In the following example the note marked by an arrow on the foreground could not have come from the C above nor the E♭ below because there is no step motion to it. In level 2, however, it is shown as an octave transfer up from a lower background line in the bass clef.

BACH: Prelude No. 2 from the *W. T. C.*, Vol. I

EXAMPLE 6

There are some octave transfers that are relatively short or do not seem to significantly affect the background lines. These may be retained for a level or two before being deleted. In the following example two octave transfers appear on level 1 and disappear on level 2:

Level 1: In the treble clef the arrow marks an octave transfer between E♭'s. The sixteenth-note figure, while highly characteristic of the piece, is relatively short and does not affect the background line enough to retain it on the next level. (The earlier E♭ in parentheses is shown simply to indicate that E♭ is still literally present while the D♭ is passing down to C.) In the bass clef an inner line goes down to the E♭ below middle C and stops. The impetus of this line is taken over by the E♭ on the top line.

Level 2: Here are two parallel neighbor motions and a brief passing motion all within the framework of treble-clef and bass-clef E♭'s.

SIMON: "Bridge Over Troubled Water," mm. 5-6

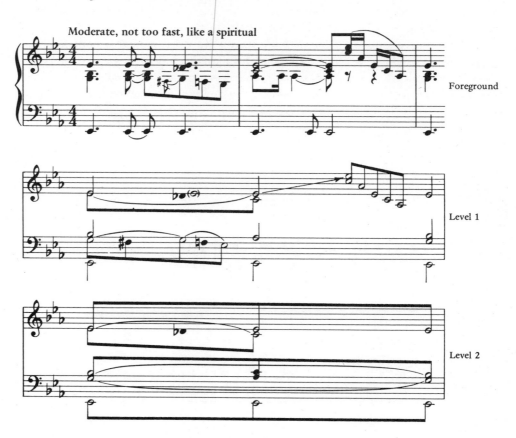

"Bridge": © 1969 Paul Simon. Used with the permission of the publisher.

EXAMPLE 7

B. MODIFICATION OF VERTICALIZATIONS THROUGH OCTAVE TRANSFER

In Chapter 10 octave transfer made possible *internal* changes within verticalizations so that fragmented lines or isolated notes could be deleted. Another important use of octave transfer is the modification of the *outer* lines or notes resulting from verticalization. We have already seen how the verticalization of bass arpeggiations is affected by octave transfer (i.e., that arpeggiated fifths lower than the roots of chords often are deleted or raised an octave when the configuration is verticalized in order to display the root as the lowest note).

The top notes resulting from the verticalization of arpeggiations are sometimes difficult to account for linearly. A judicious use of octave transfer, however, can often unravel a passage and allow one to arrive at the lines that will most adequately represent the passage.

In the following example compare the foreground to level 3. Notice particularly that the highest note on the foreground, a D, does not appear within the background lines that span the entire passage. When the arpeggiations are verticalized on level 1 the D is the highest note of the second verticalization. However, the D and the passing C are on weak beats of the measure and occupy a much shorter time span compared to the length of the entire passage.

The top-line passing motion displayed in level 3 is rhythmically emphasized by the downbeat of each measure and it spans the entire passage. Considering the top D as an octave transfer of an inner voice allows the larger passing motion (G—A—B) to be displayed as the top line—the most prominent of the linear movements in the passage.

CLEMENTI: Sonatina, Op. 36, No. 2 (3rd movement)

EXAMPLE 8

SUMMARY

When a line skips an octave it is called octave transfer. This is notated on levels with an arrow (Examples 1 and 6). However, if such a transfer is brief it may be omitted altogether (Example 3).

If top notes within verticalizations are octave transfers they may be deleted on subsequent levels so that a more important top line can be shown on the level. (Notes to be deleted should be notated with x-shaped note heads as explained in Chapter 10.)

EXERCISES FOR CHAPTER 11

1. The following passage is so clear that a level of arpeggiation is not necessary. On level 1 show the verticalizations. At two points lines transfer an octave; mark these transfers with arrows.

MOZART: Sonata in F for Piano, Four Hands (K. 497)
      (1st movement, primo piano), mm. 178-182

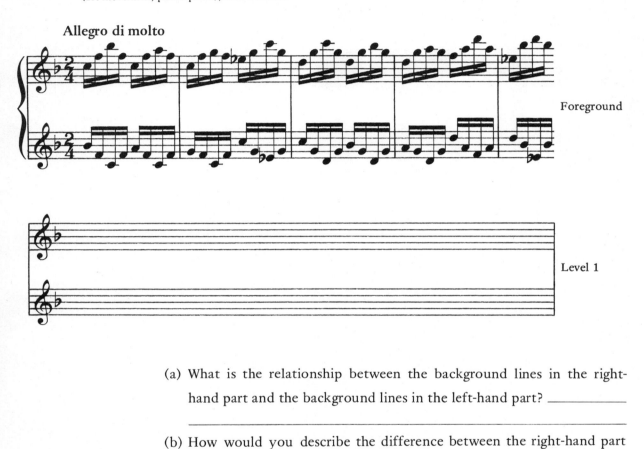

Allegro di molto

Foreground

Level 1

(a) What is the relationship between the background lines in the right-hand part and the background lines in the left-hand part? _____

_____

(b) How would you describe the difference between the right-hand part and the left-hand part? _____

_____

2. Analyze only the right-hand part of the following example. On level 1
show the arpeggiation and passing motions. Strictly speaking, there are
only two different arpeggiations; however, beam them so that there are
three. Make your decision about the beaming on the basis of the octave
transfer which you will show on the next level. On level 2 verticalize the
arpeggiations and mark the octave transfer with an arrow.

MOZART: Sonata in B♭ major for Violin and Piano (K. 454)
    (2nd movement), mm. 25-27

Foreground

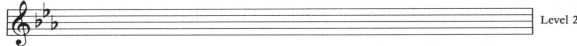

Level 1

Level 2

3. Analyze the following excerpt (it is not a segment). Use as many levels as you wish. You will find several examples of octave transfer and some incomplete neighbor motion. Be sure to carefully identify the structural dominant. It may be helpful to label the foreground chords before beginning. On the last background level the chords should be I_4^6, V_7, I.

J. STRAUSS: *Frühlingsstimmen,* Op. 410, mm. 31-39

CHAPTER 12

THE URSATZ AND OTHER MATTERS

A. THE URSATZ

Perhaps the most controversial aspect of Heinrich Schenker's[1] analysis techniques is his concept of the *Ursatz.* Schenker did not feel that a tonal composition could be reduced all the way to a single chord. The furthest background level for him was one of the figures shown in Example 1. Any of these configurations appearing on the furthest background level he called an *Ursatz,* meaning "overall structure," or "fundamental shape." There are three general types of *Ursatz* figures. They are distinguished by their interval of descent to the tonic in the top line.[2] The first type descends a third, the second descends a fifth, and the third descends an octave.

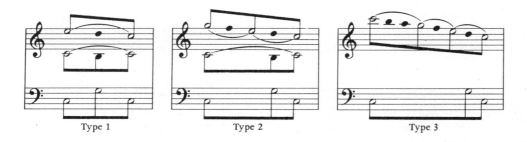

Type 1   Type 2   Type 3

EXAMPLE 1. THREE TYPES OF URSATZ

The above are slightly simplified from Schenker's originals[3] and the varieties within each type are not shown (he lists, for instance, three different descents from the fifth). They are also shown in the notation of this text, which is not the notation Schenker used.

Strictly speaking, the *Ursatz* figures underlie *only* entire compositions or movements. Segments, such as we have been analyzing, often deviate from this form, but such deviations are "normalized" by relationships to the remainder of the composition. For instance, a line that does not appear to be completed within a segment may be resumed (and completed) in the next.

1. Heinrich Schenker, mentioned in the introduction, is the music theorist upon whose works the approach of layer analysis is based.

2. The top line of an *Ursatz* is an *Urlinie.* This latter term has sometimes been used incorrectly to mean *Ursatz.*

3. See *Der Freie Satz,* Volume 3 of *Neue Musikalische Phantasien und Theorien,* Vienna, 1935; revised, 1956, pp. 50-53, and *Anhung,* Figs. 9-11, p. 2.

In that the *Ursatz* spans an entire piece it should be pointed out that major portions of the composition may be represented by single notes of this configuration. For instance, the initial *Ursatz* bass note may represent more than half of the total time of the piece. The structural dominant may represent an entire section of the piece in the key of the dominant. In a minor key the following bass line is common in the background:

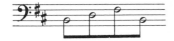

EXAMPLE 2

The second note of this configuration may represent an entire section in the key of the relative major.

Schenker was adamant in insisting that the *Ursatz* figures were indivisible and constituted the furthest possible background level. In fact (in his view), it was compulsory for one of these figures to be the furthest background level in order for the composition to be a well-formed tonal composition. A possible reason for Schenker's insistence that the *Ursatz* figures were irreduceable (i.e., to a single triad) could have been that, given the prolongation operators[4] available, configurations *other* than his *Ursatz* types could be generated from a single triad. For instance, the following, although possible foreground configurations, would not have been considered typical (or correct) background configurations for an entire composition.

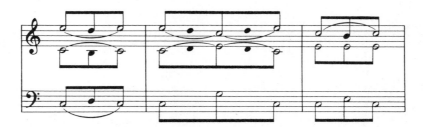

EXAMPLE 3

Thus it was perhaps more efficient for Schenker to propose a set number of *Ursatz* figures rather than write in restrictions on the operators that would prohibit the above configurations (at the level immediately prior to the single triad).

It is the author's feeling that the *Ursatz* patterns that Schenker proposed are not necessarily the only ones possible. For instance, there is some evidence to suggest that the first Prelude in the *Well-Tempered Clavier* proceeds 3—2—3, rather than 3—2—1. For those pieces that may not be traditionally tonal, figures such as those in Example 3 may, in fact, be a distinguishing factor stylistically.

While one may not insist on the appearance of one of the *Ursatz* figures in the furthest background, they nevertheless embody general concepts that

4. See Chapter 6, Section C.

are helpful in an analysis. First of all there is a sense in which a descending line tends to finalize, or "close out," a passage. It is even common for notes "left hanging" in an antecedent phrase to be picked up and brought down in a consequent phrase.

Of more importance than the upper line of the *Ursatz* is the structural bass. This arpeggiation is necessary no matter what the upper lines are. There is probably no more important motion in the background than this for segment definition and coherence in the large.

B. EVALUATION THROUGH ANALYSIS

Evaluation of an art work on the basis of analysis is fraught with problems. In the case of music, however, several observations can be made. First of all, one would probably not want to attempt the comparison (for evaluative purposes) of widely disparate works (such as deciding whether a specific rag were "better" than a specific symphony). The number of relationships and their type should probably determine the major categories of compositions for evaluative purposes. Then *within* each group the number and type of relationships could help in further evaluation or comparison.

A definitive factor in terms of interest seems to be a multiplicity of function such as a single note serving different functions at several different levels of the piece. This does not necessarily mean that the music must appear complex. A clever use of relatively simple pitch and rhythmic relationships can leave room for many different interpretations of a passage. This kind of multiplicity musicians and "advanced" listeners find interesting. (For further discussion of this point see Chapter 7, Section A, and Chapter 8, Section D.)

A final word of caution is in order. No analytical system is as sophisticated as an intelligent listener. If your ear tells you one thing and your analysis tells you another, trust your ear.

C. RHYTHM

The most serious problem of layer analysis is the absence of a sufficient formulation of the rhythmic component. Schenker maintained that rhythm did not exist on background levels; however, in making decisions about the structural weight of specific notes he often evoked rhythmic considerations. Whether it is practical to include rhythmical elements within background levels or to apply rhythmic transformations as a separate process is a genuine problem in layer analysis. Recent work seems to indicate that the former is possible.

Until such time as rhythm is better incorporated into layer analysis, the evoking of rhythm for the purposes of an analysis will be somewhat *ad hoc,* but one must do so nevertheless. In fact, it would be quite impossible to arrive at a meaningful analysis without taking into consideration at least the obvious emphasis that rhythm gives to some notes in context.

D. RELATIONSHIP OF LAYER ANALYSIS TO FORM

While layer analysis displays the inner counterpoint of a composition, it does not generally tell a great deal about the form. Many people, confusing the two, expect any kind of analysis to address problems of form. Although major subdivisions of a piece may be represented by single notes in a far background level, it is also meaningful to identify such sections as recapitulation or subordinate theme, etc. The relationship between layer analysis and form will probably be greatly clarified after an adequate theory of rhythm has been incorporated into analysis techniques of this type.

E. ANALYZING ON YOUR OWN

The first rule when doing analyses is to *use your ear.* If possible, play the piece or segment many times before you begin (or at least listen to it repeatedly). As a next step it may be helpful to label the chords. (The more complex the passage, the more necessary this step becomes.) Tonal music can be very complex, and you will encounter situations not explicitly covered in this text. The notation is extensible, however, to cover most of these. For a few examples see Appendix A.

As has been mentioned before, do not expect to move smoothly from one level to the next. You will have to back up and start some layers over several times before deciding which interpretation best suits your conception of the piece. Also, do not expect to find the same number of levels present throughout a composition. Some sections will be more complex than others and thus require more levels. Even individual lines within the same section may require a different number of levels for their analysis (i.e., upper lines are often more complex than bass lines).

And finally, the analysis you arrive at should represent the way you hear the piece. Do not settle for a manipulation of the notation. Music analysis is not of the visual, it is of the aural.

FINAL EXERCISES

Analyze the following segments using as many levels as you like. In that none of these are complete pieces the *Ursatz* forms are not applicable; however, the structural bass arpeggiation will be present. It is not necessary to reduce beyond the level on which the structural bass is displayed.

1. In this example not all passing motion is between members of the tonic triad (despite the reiterated D in the bass). Measure 3, for instance, is a prolongation of the dominant.

BEETHOVEN: Six Variations for Piano, Op. 76

2. This example consists of two four-measure phrases (segments). The bass
for the two (combined) is I—V—I—V—I. Show this arpeggiation in the final
level. Notice in measure 3 that there is an octave transfer.

HANDEL: Suite No. 10 (Menuetto, var. 1)

3. The lowest notes in measures 2 and 3 are pedal notes. Pedal notes are notes that are retained in the bass (repeated or held) which no longer function as bass notes. These should be deleted at some level. (Use the x-shaped note heads.)

LISZT: Polonaise No. I, mm. 70-73

4. The top background line of this example consists of a descent from the
   fifth scale degree to the tonic. On the foreground notice the next to last
   note in the right-hand part. Such a note is usually called an escape tone.
   It is, in fact, an anticipation of the C harmony that follows in the last
   measure. Notate the E as an arpeggiated note with the final C, but in a
   subsequent level delete it as an octave transfer.

CLEMENTI: Sonatina, Op. 36, No. 5 (2nd movement)

5. There are many octave transfers in this example.

SCHUBERT: Waltz, Op. 9, No. 3

APPENDIX A

LAYER NOTATION

The notation used in this text (combined with the greater number of levels it necessitates) is believed by the author to be clearer with respect to the assignation of contrapuntal function than that used by Schenker and other writers. This clarity is particularly helpful in teaching layer analysis on an elementary level. However, the notation is also extensible and appropriate to analyses of greater length and complexity than those presented in this volume.

Levels contain no time signatures or internal bar lines. A bar, however, should appear at the beginning and end of each level. No brace should be used on the initial bar line.

No time values or durations are expressed on levels. The color of the note head (white or black), the beaming, and the slurring indicate the contrapuntal function of the note *within a specific level.* The parts of a note configuration are as follows:

The following are the primary notations of layer analysis:

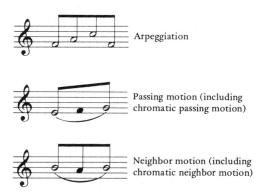

Notes within extensive passing motions can be notated as arpeggiated notes if they receive some rhythmic articulation or if there is a need for such an indication.

as opposed to

Variants of neighbor motion are as follows:

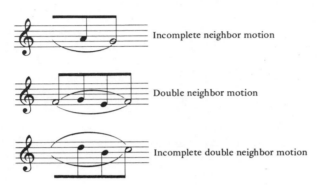

Incomplete neighbor motion

Double neighbor motion

Incomplete double neighbor motion

The initial or final note of a neighbor motion may be subordinated by using a black note head:

Any of the above may be embedded within a larger arpeggiation. A change in the direction of the stemming can be helpful in differentiating the various motions:

One motion may be intercepted by another:

Passing notes between members of different arpeggiations are notated only with the black note head and slur:

A suspension may be notated:

An anticipation may be notated:

Notes to be deleted in the subsequent level because of octave duplication are notated with an x-shaped note head. The arrow indicates the note being duplicated:

Octave transfer is indicated with an arrow:

Notations that should span relatively long sections can be segmented in the following way:

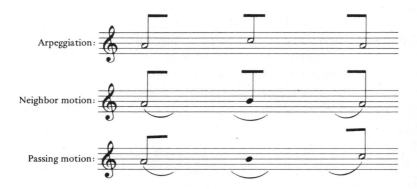

APPENDIX B

DIVERGENCES WITH SCHENKER

The divergences in this text from some of the techniques employed by Schenker are primarily for the purpose of a more efficient presentation of layer analysis at elementary pedagogical levels. However, in order to avoid misrepresenting Schenker (particularly since most of his works remain unpublished in English), at least brief elaboration with respect to these differences is necessary.

First of all, Schenker did not use the term "layer analysis." I do not recall who first suggested this term to me, but it seems far more satisfactory than "graphic analysis" or "Schenkerian analysis."

Concerning the format of the analyses, Schenker used a reverse of the layout employed in this text; he placed the *Ursatz* at the top of the page and the foreground on the bottom. Furthermore, his foreground was not the composition itself, but an immediately underlying level.[1]

In differentiating levels Schenker used the terms "foreground" (*Vordergrund*), "middle ground" (*Mittelgrund*), and "background" (*Hintergrund*). I have used only foreground and background.

Schenker used far fewer levels than I have indicated were necessary,[2] and for this reason packed a great deal of information into each. The number of relationships per level this necessitates makes Schenker's analyses difficult to employ in elementary classroom teaching. Schenker used few levels probably because his analyses were not intended for novices and because the analysis of an entire composition could otherwise take an inordinate number of levels.

Schenker differentiated between many different contrapuntal configurations, indicating them partly through the notation and partly through verbal instructions or abbreviations. I have generalized these to three primary functions and differentiated them entirely by means of the notation.

Partly because of the increased number of levels employed and partly because of the clarity of the notation, the relationships between levels in the method here presented are generally more obvious than is the case with Schenker's analyses. In particular, I think they are clearer with respect

---

1. See also Chapter 12, Section A.

2. To be more specific, he usually used four or five levels, but those levels would represent the analysis of a complete movement, not just a few measures as has been shown here.

to which notes are to be deleted and which are to be retained from level to level. As students begin to analyze on their own they may, of course, omit the more obvious levels, thus reducing to manageable size the analysis of lengthy passages.

Interruption technique has been omitted because it seemed beyond the scope of an elementary text. It should, however, be among the first items considered in a further study of layer analysis.

APPENDIX C

SUPPLEMENTARY READINGS

The following is a list of books and articles that will provide supplementary reading in layer analysis. Each of them deserves to be read in its entirety; however, as time is usually a factor, page numbers are given to indicate the most pertinent sections of longer works. All of the sources listed are in English, which accounts for the fact that only one work by Schenker himself is included. Those sources that contain analyses do not employ the same notation as that used in this text. (See Appendix A.)

Babbitt, Milton. Review of Salzer's "Structural Hearing." *Journal of the American Musicological Society,* 5, no. 3 (Fall 1952): 262.

Beach, David. "A Schenker Bibliography." *Journal of Music Theory,* 13, no. 1 (Spring 1969): 2-26.

Forte, Allen. "Schenker's Conception of Musical Structure." *Journal of Music Theory,* 3, no. 1 (April 1959): 1-30.

Komar, Arthur J. *Theory of Suspensions: A Study of Metrical and Pitch Relations in Tonal Music.* Princeton: Princeton University Press, 1971. Chapter 2 (through no. 2, pp. 11-28), p. 4, 30-35 (see also p. 165).

Salzer, Felix, and Schachter, Carl. *Counterpoint in Composition: The Study of Voice Leading.* New York: McGraw-Hill, 1969. Introduction and pp. 153-171.

Salzer, Felix. *Structural Hearing: Tonal Coherence in Music.* New York: Charles Boni, 1952. Introduction and pp. 3-31, 257-261.

Schenker, Heinrich. *Five Graphic Musical Analyses.* New York: Dover, 1969. Introduction (by Felix Salzer, pp. 13-16), Glossary (by Felix Salzer, pp. 23-26), Analysis of Bach: Prelude No. 1 in C major (*Well-Tempered Clavier,* vol. 1), pp. 36-37.

TEAR-OUT EXERCISES

EXERCISES FOR CHAPTER 1

1. After the deletion of repeated notes the bottom background line of this passage can be represented as a sustained G, as shown in the layer below. Using eighth notes, add the top background line above the sustained G. The first two notes are already given.

BACH: Suite No. 3 for Cello (Gigue), mm. 25-31

2. There are two background lines present in the following example: one stationary and one moving. Write both on the layer below. You will have to use tied whole notes and quarter notes. The first note in each line is given.

MOZART: Sonata in E minor for Violin and Piano (K. 304)
  (1st movement), mm. 104-107

3. In this example both background lines are moving. Write each on the layer below. The first two notes in each line are given.

DOMENICO SCARLATTI: Sonata No. 9, mm. 27-28

4. In the next example there are three background lines. A separate staff is provided for the notation of each (although all three combine to form the layer). The first note of each line is already given; fill in the remaining notes using only dotted quarters. Tie notes where necessary.

MOZART: Sonata in G for Violin and Piano (K. 301)
      (2nd movement), mm. 37-40

5. In this example there are four lines present (counting the bass line). In the layer below write the upper three lines (where indicated) using dotted half notes. The bass line is already given as well as the first note of each of the other lines. Tie notes where necessary.

ARTHUR FOOTE: Twenty Preludes, No. 3, mm. 3-5

6. In this measure the treble-clef part contains two lines: a line beginning on the D above middle C, and a stationary D on the octave above. On the layer fill in the moving line (marked with an arrow). You will need to use quarter notes and eighth notes. The first note is given.

BACH: Pastorale in F major, m. 33

In the above exercise, what is the relationship between the pitches of the line you filled in and the pitches of the line just below it?_____
_____

EXERCISES IN CHORD AND INTERVAL RECOGNITION

This chapter consists entirely of exercises which review chord and interval recognition.

A. CHORD IDENTIFICATION AND INTERVALLIC STRUCTURE

1. Label each chord with Roman numerals (indicating the chord within the key) and Arabic numeral subscripts to indicate inversion (e.g., I, I_6, I_4^6, etc.). Label the chords in the first line as if they were in D major and those in the second line as if they were in A minor.

In D major:____

In A minor:____

2. Label the intervals marked within the following chords. Reduce each interval name to within an octave (e.g., major 10th = major 3rd). Use the abbreviations "maj." and "min."

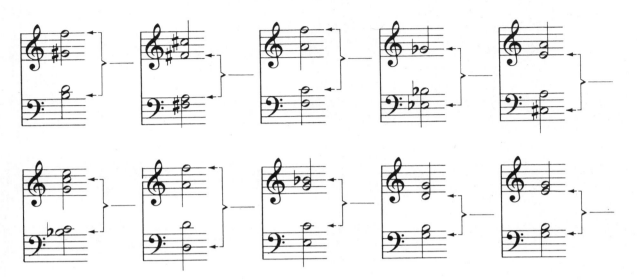

3. The initial measures of many melodies are often made up of notes from a single chord. In the space provided write the name of the chord to which the bracketed notes belong.

(a) MOZART: *The Magic Flute* (beginning)

chord:____

(b) SCHUBERT: *The Post* (beginning)

chord:____

(c) MOZART: *Bastien and Bastienne* (beginning)

chord:____

B. RECOGNITION OF CHORDS IN CONTEXT

1. Chords are easiest to identify when they appear in "block" form, as in the following example. Write the chord names (using Roman numerals) in the blanks below the staves.

BEETHOVEN: Sonata, Op. 14, No. 2 (2nd movement)

2. In the following example the bass note appears on the beat and the rest of the chord one-half beat later. Write the chord names, as before, in the blanks provided.

SCHUBERT: "By the River" ("Auf dem Flusse")

3. Sometimes chords appear in arpeggiated form (i.e., the notes of the chord are presented one at a time, not in block form nor "rolled"). In the following example a bracket is used to mark off the area, or "domain," of each chord. In the blank staves below write the chords (one for each bracket) with half notes in block form. Two are already given. Then write the names of the chords (using Roman numerals) in the blanks provided.

BEETHOVEN: Sonata, Op. 13 (3rd movement), mm. 109-112

4. Analyze the following example as directed.

   (a) Indicate the domain of each chord with brackets under the bass clef (as was done for you in the previous example). The first bracket is given.

   (b) On the staff below write out the chords for the left-hand part (the bass-clef part) in block form. Use whole notes. The first chord is given.

   (c) Write the chord names (using Roman numerals) in the blanks provided.

MOZART: Fantasia in C minor (K. 475), mm. 62-70

5. In this example only write the chord names with letters of the alphabet (A maj., E♭ min., etc.) rather than Roman numerals. Use the blanks provided. Do not show inversion.

PAUL SIMON: "A Poem on the Underground Wall," mm. 45-48

6. By writing the arpeggiations in block chords and deleting repeated notes you should be able to reduce the following entire passage to only two chords.

(a) Mark a bracket under the domain of each chord.

(b) Write the chords on the blank staves below.

BACH: *Twelve Little Preludes,* No. 3

EXERCISES FOR CHAPTER 3

1. (a) In the bass-clef part there are two background lines. Circle the notes that make up the bottom line. (The first note is already circled.)

   (b) Write this line in eighth notes on the blank staff below.

MENDELSSOHN: *Songs Without Words,* Op. 19, No. 2 (beginning)

2. The following melody contains two parallel background lines. Write them on the staff below. Use only half notes and whole notes. Tie notes where necessary.

PAUL SIMON: "A Poem on the Underground Wall," mm. 45-48

3. This example shows a clear arpeggiation of three lines. Write these lines on the staff below. The first notes are already given.

BEETHOVEN: Sonata, Op. 81a
  (3rd movement, "Le Retour"), mm. 176-181

4. At two places in the following example a single line splits into two lines. At each point where this occurs circle the two notes that result.

BEETHOVEN: Sonata, Op. 31, No. 1 (3rd movement), mm. 29-31

5. Write each of the arpeggiations as block chords on the blank staff below. With arrows show any splitting or merging of lines (as was done in Example 5).

BEETHOVEN: Sonata, Op. 2, No. 1 (4th movement), m. 170

6. (a) The following example contains seven background lines. Write them on
the staves indicated. The first notes in each line are given.

MENDELSSOHN: *Songs Without Words,* Op. 53, No. 3, mm. 96-99

(b) What is the relationship between the arpeggiated lines and the treble-
clef lines? _____

7. In the following passage three lines are being arpeggiated. Write them on the blank staff provided.

BACH: Partita No. 3 for Unaccompanied Violin, mm. 20-22

(a) In which measure does the suspension occur?_____

(b) To what note does the suspended note resolve?_____

EXERCISES FOR CHAPTER 4

1. Analyze the following measure from a Bach organ prelude as instructed at each level, then answer questions (a) and (b).

BACH: Prelude and Fugue in G major, m. 8

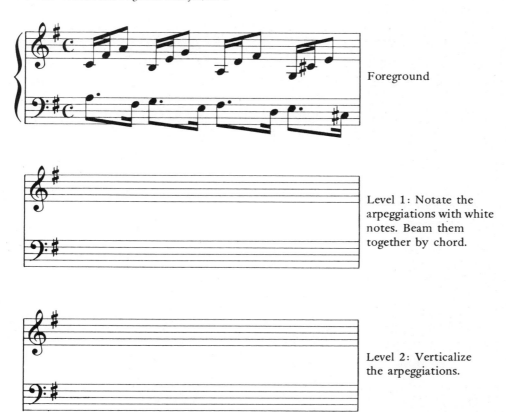

Foreground

Level 1: Notate the arpeggiations with white notes. Beam them together by chord.

Level 2: Verticalize the arpeggiations.

(a) In the background line of level 2 to what note does the first bass-clef F♯ move? _____

(b) In level 2 how are the top two and bottom two lines related?_____

_____

2. Analyze as instructed on each level, then answer (a) and (b).

MOZART: Sonata in C (K. 309), mm. 35-36

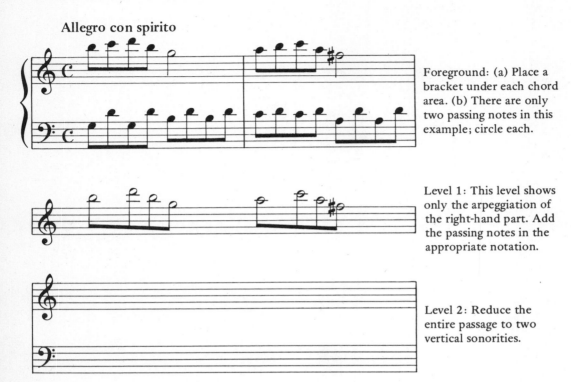

Foreground: (a) Place a bracket under each chord area. (b) There are only two passing notes in this example; circle each.

Level 1: This level shows only the arpeggiation of the right-hand part. Add the passing notes in the appropriate notation.

Level 2: Reduce the entire passage to two vertical sonorities.

(a) In the background lines of level 2, to what note does the bass note G (in the first chord) move? _____

(b) In level 2, to what note does the treble note G (in the first chord) move? _____

3. Reduce the following passage as instructed on each level, then answer a) and b).

MOZART: Sonata in F for Piano, Four Hands (K. 497)
       (1st movement, primo piano), mm. 197-199

Foreground: Circle every passing note.

Level 1: Add the passing notes using the correct notation.

Level 2: Show the arpeggiations as vertical sonorities.

(a) In level 2, *to* what note does the first F move? _____

(b) In level 2, *from* what note does the last F come? _____

4. Analyze as instructed on each level.

HANDEL: Suite No. 1 (Allemande), mm. 17-19

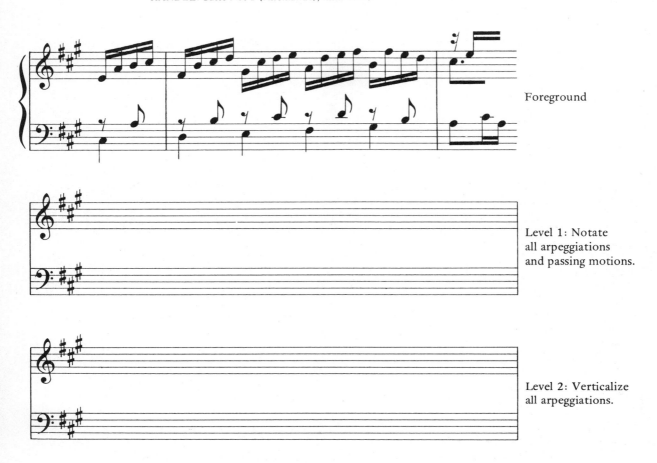

Foreground

Level 1: Notate
all arpeggiations
and passing motions.

Level 2: Verticalize
all arpeggiations.

(a) In level 2, to what note does the bass-clef D in the fourth verticalization go? _____

(b) What grounds would one have for claiming that there was a sense in which that same D (in level 2) was present in the fifth verticalization?

_____

EXERCISES FOR CHAPTER 5

1. Analyze the following melody as instructed at each level.

Foreground: Place a bracket underneath each chord area (there are only four) and circle each neighbor note.

Level 1: This level shows only the arpeggiations. Add the neighbor notes using the correct notation.

Level 2: Reduce the entire passage to four vertical sonorities, then add arrows to show the background lines (as was done in Example 5 of this chapter).

BACH: Suite No. 1 for Cello (Prelude)

(a) Does the top line of level 2 consist of (check one):

☐ neighbor motion

☐ passing motion

(b) Does the middle line of level 2 consist of (check one):

☐ neighbor motion

☐ passing motion

(c) If there were another level below level 2 it would consist of a single chord. The chord would be (check one):

☐ C major

☐ G major

☐ D major

2. Analyze the following passage as instructed.

(a) The treble-clef line of level 1 gives only some of the arpeggiated notes. Add all the remaining notes from the foreground using the correct notation.

(b) Write out the bass-clef part of the analysis in its entirety. The beaming in the treble-clef part is to distinguish the two phrases; preserve this same beaming in the bass-clef part.

(c) The entire passage could be reduced to a single chord. What is that chord? _____

BACH: Two-part Inventions, No. 8

Foreground

Level 1

3. The following exercise gives the foreground and most of the second level of a four-measure fragment.

   (a) On the foreground put a bracket under each chord area and label with letter names (do not show inversions), e.g., ⌞⎯⎯⌟ ⌞⎯⎯⌟

                                                        D maj.   E min.

   (b) On level 1 write in the bass-clef arpeggiations. Beam all the notes in the same chord together.

   (c) On level 1 notate the treble-clef part, correctly showing arpeggiations, neighbor notes, and passing notes. Beam the notes of the arpeggiations together by chord. The C in (foreground) measure 3 will have to be notated as an isolated passing note between two different arpeggiations.

   (d) Level 2 verticalizes the arpeggiations of level 1. The bottom two lines in the bass clef are large-scale neighbor motions. Add the two black note heads (for these neighbor notes) to the empty stem marked with an arrow.

   (e) If there were another level below level 2 it would consist of one chord.

   What would that chord be? _____

CLEMENTI: Sonatina, Op. 36, No. 3 (2nd movement)

4. The following example contains a neighbor to a note which is itself a neighbor. Analyze the passage as instructed at each level. Do not notate the upper note of the trill.

HANDEL: Suite No. 6 (Gigue)

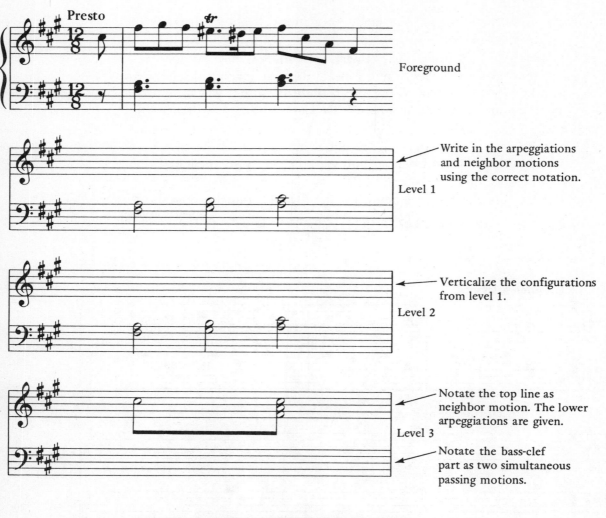

Foreground

Write in the arpeggiations and neighbor motions using the correct notation.

Level 1

Verticalize the configurations from level 1.

Level 2

Notate the top line as neighbor motion. The lower arpeggiations are given.

Level 3

Notate the bass-clef part as two simultaneous passing motions.

(a) What note is a neighbor of a neighbor? _____

(b) If the passage were reduced one more level it would be a single configuration. What would that configuration be? _____

EXERCISES FOR CHAPTER 7

1. Analyze this fragment as directed for each level.

    Level 1: Show only arpeggiations. Each will contain two notes.

    Level 2: Verticalize the arpeggiations.

    Level 3: Notate the neighbor motions. The sustained line is already given.

    Level 4: Delete the neighbor motions and notate a passing motion.

MOZART: Sonata in F (K. 332)
        (3rd movement), mm. 3-4

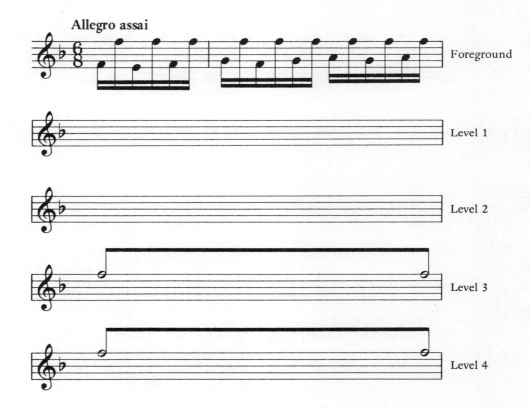

2. Analyze only the bass-clef part on each level as instructed.

Level 1: Notate the arpeggiations.

Level 2: Verticalize the arpeggiations.

Level 3: Two bass-clef staves are given on which to indicate the background lines (of the bass-clef part). Notate the bottom two lines on the bottom staff and the top two on the top staff.

BEETHOVEN: Bagatelles, Op. 119, No. 3, mm. 42-45

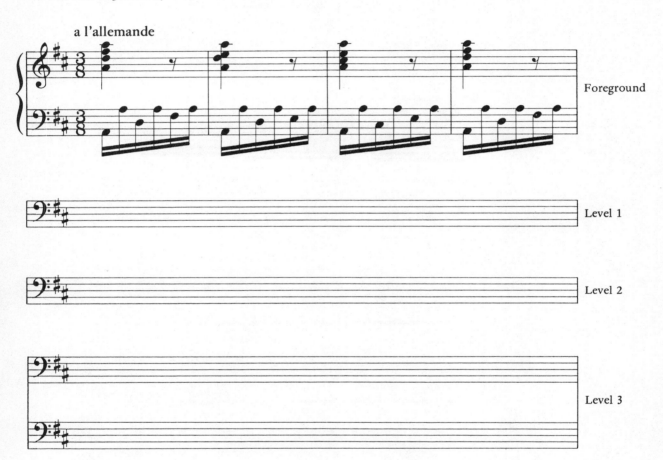

3. Analyze as directed for each level.

Level 1: Notate the arpeggiations.

Level 2: Verticalize the arpeggiations.

Level 3: Often the background lines of upper parts are more complex than the background lines underlying lower parts. In this example the treble-clef parts require one more level of reduction than the bass-clef parts. On this level show only the treble-clef parts. Notate *only* two background lines. The top should consist of a string of neighbor motions, the bottom a passing motion. All other notes may be deleted.

Level 4: The bass line is given. Notate the remaining three moving lines that span this example.

BEETHOVEN: Variations on "Nel cor più non mi sento" (var. 6)

Foreground

Level 1

Level 2

Level 3

Level 4

EXERCISES FOR CHAPTER 8

1. Complete the notation of the top background line in level 1. Notice that the last C♯ in measure one receives no rhythmic emphasis and is thus not notated as a part of the arpeggiation. There is one incomplete neighbor.

SCARLATTI: Sonata No. 23 (Longo 238), mm. 1-3

2. In the following example some of the arpeggiation is given in level 1. Add all of the remaining notes (including arpeggiations) using the correct notation.

JOPLIN: *A Breeze from Alabama*, mm. 5-6

3. In the following example the complete bass part is given on level 1. Within it there are two E's (marked with arrows) that could be mistaken for incomplete neighbor notes. Notice that they are shown on the level to be *complete* neighbors, although in each case the initial note of the neighbor motion is not immediately adjacent to the remainder of the configuration.

There are, however, two genuine incomplete neighbors in the treble-clef part. On level 1 the stationary line (on middle C) is already given. Add the remaining notes of the treble-clef part in the correct notation.

TELEMANN: Fantasia No. 2

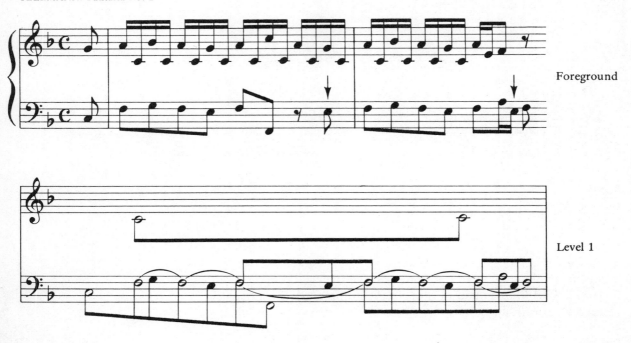

Foreground

Level 1

4. On level 1 notate only the treble-clef part of the following example.

HANDEL: Passacaglia

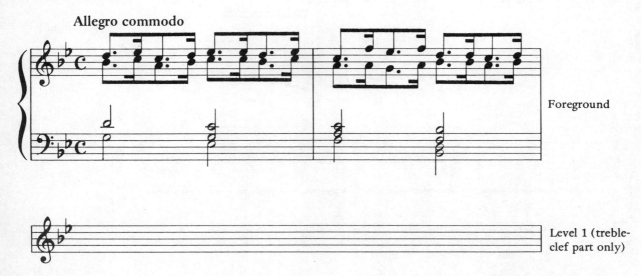

Foreground

Level 1 (treble-clef part only)

5. Notate completely level 1 of the following passage. There is one chromatic passing note, one chromatic neighbor note, and one incomplete neighbor. The treble-clef notation should show the arpeggiation of a B♭ chord in the first (foreground) measure and an F⁶ chord in the second (foreground) measure.

MOZART: Piano Sonata in B♭ (K. 570) (3rd movement)

In the second measure of the above example an incomplete neighbor interrupts a passing motion. What is the passing *note* of that motion?_____

6. Analyze only the treble-clef part on the level provided.

FRIEDLAW: Sonata No. 2

With the exception of the last note, the melody of this example contains exactly the same notes as the Clementi example, the third exercise in Chapter 5. How does the background of the treble-clef part differ from that of the Clementi example? What specific events in *this* example caused those differences? _____

_____

EXERCISES FOR CHAPTER 9

1. The following passage is similar to Examples 1 and 2 within this chapter. Analyze as instructed for each level.

Level 1: Show all arpeggiations (deleting any adjacent repeated notes) and neighbor and passing notes. The first configurations are given.

Level 2: Delete the passing and neighbor notes and verticalize the arpeggiations.

Level 3: Notate the background lines. The structural I—V—I should appear on this level. A stationary line on the E above middle C may be omitted.

HANDEL: *Seven Pieces,* No. 3, mm. 21-22

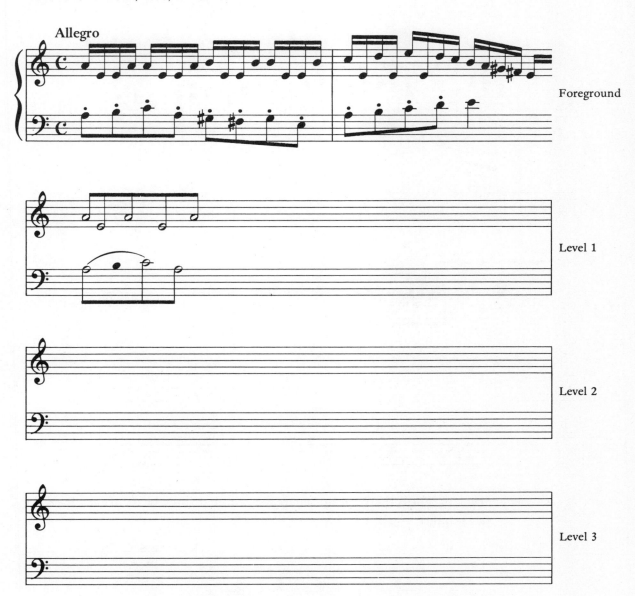

2. Analyze as instructed for each level.

Level 1: The bass notes are given. Add the upper lines. A few notes are already given. At this level the upper lines should only show arpeggiation and passing motion.

Level 2: Verticalize the arpeggiations and notate the longer-range neighbor motions and passing motions in the upper lines. The initial neighbor motions are already given.

Level 3: On the bottom staff notate the structural bass arpeggiation (with the addition of an incomplete neighbor). On the top staff notate the two background lines that span the length of the entire passage.

GOTTSCHALK: *Miserere du Trovatore,* Op. 52, mm. 33-36

What reason is there for not analyzing the first three beats of measure 2 in the following way? _____

_____

3. The following example contains a background I—V motion in the bass. Blank staves are provided for your analysis. Use two or three levels as needed. On the final level show the bass arpeggiation without neighbor notes or passing notes.

HANDEL: Suite No. 9 ("Gigue")

4. In the I—V—I bass movement any of the chords may appear in inversion. In the following example the dominant is in inversion making the structural bass line a neighbor motion (I—V$_6$—I). Analyze as instructed for each level.

Level 1: Display all arpeggiation, neighbor and passing motion.

Level 2: Verticalize all arpeggiations. In addition show the B♭ as a passing note (between two notes that are not members of the same arpeggiation).

Level 3: On the bottom staff show the bass line and the line above it (beginning on the A below middle C). On the middle staff show the line that starts on middle C. On the top staff show the top two lines.

BEETHOVEN: Sonata, Op. 2, No. 1 (Trio)

EXERCISES FOR CHAPTER 10

1. On level 1 notate the lines underlying the following foreground, but in each case of a line doubled at the octave delete one line. Distribute the remaining lines among the three staves provided. (This example is simple enough that a level using the x-shaped note heads is not necessary.)

CHOPIN: Preludes, Op. 28, No. 20

2. Analyze as instructed for each level.

Level 1: Verticalize the arpeggiations. (Show the neighbors as single notes.)

Level 2: Indicate the octave duplications (within the verticalizations) with x-shaped note heads and arrows.

Level 3: Notate the four remaining background lines. Each consists of neighbor motion. (If you have more than four lines, you did not show enough octave duplications in level 2.)

CHOPIN: Preludes, Op. 28, No. 1

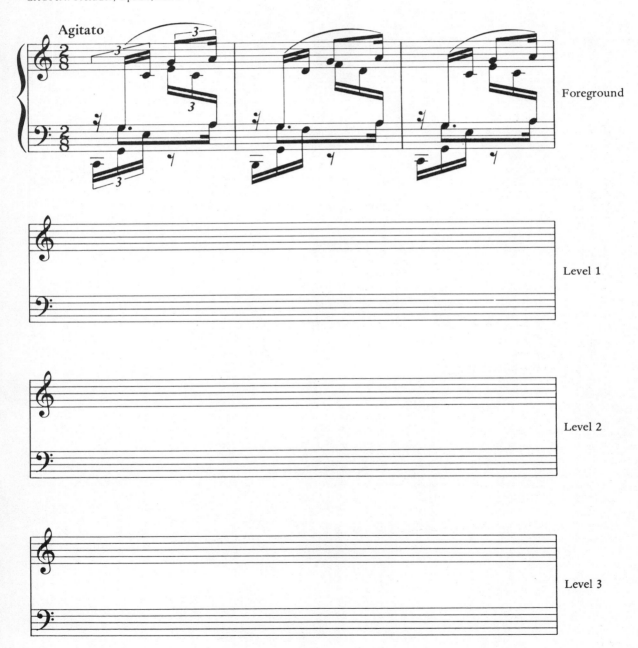

3. On each of the levels the bass-clef parts are already given. Add the treble-clef parts. In level 2 show the deletion of a fragmentary duplication of one of the descending bass-clef lines (using x-shaped note heads and arrows).

BEETHOVEN: Sonata, Op. 79 (3rd movement)

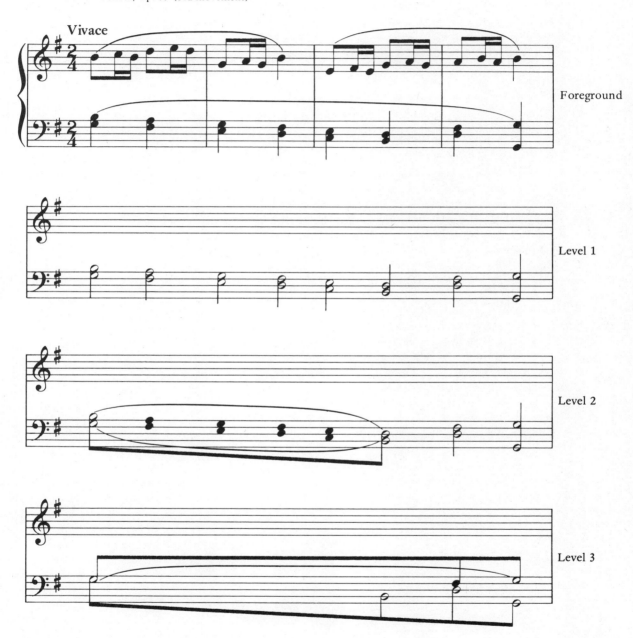

EXERCISES FOR CHAPTER 11

1. The following passage is so clear that a level of arpeggiation is not necessary. On level 1 show the verticalizations. At two points lines transfer an octave; mark these transfers with arrows.

MOZART: Sonata in F for Piano, Four Hands (K. 497)
(1st movement, primo piano), mm. 178-182

(a) What is the relationship between the background lines in the right-hand part and the background lines in the left-hand part? _____

_____

(b) How would you describe the difference between the right-hand part and the left-hand part? _____

_____

2. Analyze only the right-hand part of the following example. On level 1 show the arpeggiation and passing motions. Strictly speaking, there are only two different arpeggiations; however, beam them so that there are three. Make your decision about the beaming on the basis of the octave transfer which you will show on the next level. On level 2 verticalize the arpeggiations and mark the octave transfer with an arrow.

MOZART: Sonata in B♭ major for Violin and Piano (K. 454)
(2nd movement), mm. 25-27

3. Analyze the following excerpt (it is not a segment). Use as many levels as you wish. You will find several examples of octave transfer and some incomplete neighbor motion. Be sure to carefully identify the structural dominant. It may be helpful to label the foreground chords before beginning. On the last background level the chords should be I_4^6, V_7, I.

J. STRAUSS: *Frühlingsstimmen*, Op. 410, mm. 31-39

Tempo di Valse

FINAL EXERCISES

Analyze the following segments using as many levels as you like. In that none of these are complete pieces the *Ursatz* forms are not applicable; however, the structural bass arpeggiation will be present. It is not necessary to reduce beyond the level on which the structural bass is displayed.

1. In this example not all passing motion is between members of the tonic triad (despite the reiterated D in the bass). Measure 3, for instance, is a prolongation of the dominant.

BEETHOVEN: Six Variations for Piano, Op. 76

2. This example consists of two four-measure phrases (segments). The bass for the two (combined) is I—V—I—V—I. Show this arpeggiation in the final level. Notice in measure 3 that there is an octave transfer.

HANDEL: Suite No. 10 (Menuetto, var. 1)

3. The lowest notes in measures 2 and 3 are pedal notes. Pedal notes are notes that are retained in the bass (repeated or held) which no longer function as bass notes. These should be deleted at some level. (Use the x-shaped note heads.)

LISZT: Polonaise No. I, mm. 70-73

4. The top background line of this example consists of a descent from the fifth scale degree to the tonic. On the foreground notice the next to last note in the right-hand part. Such a note is usually called an escape tone. It is, in fact, an anticipation of the C harmony that follows in the last measure. Notate the E as an arpeggiated note with the final C, but in a subsequent level delete it as an octave transfer.

CLEMENTI: Sonatina, Op. 36, No. 5 (2nd movement)

Allegro moderato

5. There are many octave transfers in this example.

SCHUBERT: Waltz, Op. 9, No. 3

INDEX